ELIZA SCALIA

The Fury of Tigerclaw

The Adventures of Silver Dove, Book Two

Eliza Scalia

Cover Illustration by:
Suji Gallianetti

Dedicated to all of the bullies in my past and present, for they provided the inspiration for these books.

Chapter One

Colomba-
The New Normal

My body flies through the air and slams into the wall of my classroom, knocking the breath out of me. Everything aches, it feels as if my body has been bashed around for hours by a professional boxer. I can't even feel a part of me that doesn't hurt. My vision doubles and spins from when my head hit the wall. I almost want to puke from the nauseating feeling in my head. Even though my vision is messed up I can still see the chaos around me. Papers swirl around me in a storm-like breeze while demonic shadow dogs run around me, chasing my friends who are screaming in terror, trying to get away from the horrible monsters. The shadow dogs bark and growl, flashing their fangs at everyone while all the people scream, creating a horrific noise that makes my ears ring. None of the dogs come after me though, something more sinister has chosen me as its prey. Above me is a person clothed all in black, with a bird-like mask on his face and black wings coming out of his back, the Crow.

"You should have just given up Silver Dove." The Crow says above me while he smirks. "I will never give in, the only way you can win is to join me." He holds out his hand to me and I understand what he means. I can either take his hand and join him, or I can lose and probably die by his hands.

Using all of my strength, I lift my hand up to him, my hand quivers with weakness. The Crow's eyes grow wide in excitement beneath his mask, eager for me to take his hand. Even though that is what he wants, and what would save me, instead I slap his hand away from me, my face set with an angered determination. The Crow scowls at me. In his eyes I can see what he is thinking. He thinks that I have made a stupid decision and he is going to make me regret it.

I try to pick myself off the ground, I need to get up, I need to fight back and defend everyone, but I am now too weak and injured to even get on my feet. I fall back on the ground while the Crow laughs at me, enjoying the fact that I am in pain. I look up at him to try and beg him to stop this, to let everyone be, but I can tell that it would be useless to try. What he said is true, he will never give up.

He lifts his staff high into the air so that he can hit me across the face, but something stops him. I take in a gasp of air and I nearly fly out of my bed, my heart racing like a speeding car. I look around to see that I am still in my bedroom, it was only a nightmare. I bury my face in my hands, groaning softly, wanting nothing more than to forget about that horrible dream.

It has been a few weeks since the Crow attacked our school and I fought against him along with his army of demonic shadow dogs. Even though I won, I have been having these nightmares almost every night. It's as if my mind keeps wanting to remind me about his promise to return, to keep me prepared for whatever he has planned. Rubbing my eyes, I look at my alarm clock to see that I have only about ten minutes until it will go off. No point in laying down again, so I start getting ready for school.

Everything at school seems to be returning to normal, but everyone is still on edge, all of us aware that the Crow promised that he would return to cause more mayhem. He told us that he was going to take care of the bullies in our school and make sure that it is safe for everyone. He was making himself out to be a hero when he was attacking the school, that doesn't make any sense. I have to fight against a crazy person.

After the battle happened, the Crow and Silver Dove have been the only things people can talk about. Everyone is wondering who they are. It is almost flattering to hear so many people talking about me, but nobody knows that I am the one they are talking about since nobody at school knows my secret. For a moment, I wonder what it would be like for everyone to know that I am Silver Dove, to have people admire me for what I have done and cheer me on so that my next battle with the Crow won't be as scary. I know that I will have everyone's support. Of course, I know I can't do that, if everyone knew who I am, then that would also mean that the Crow would know my identity and ruin my entire life. He would probably attack my family too considering how evil he is. Who knows what someone as crazy as him would do if he found out who I really am. I could probably just kiss my entire life goodbye if he ever found out my identity.

As soon as I have gotten dressed and ready for the day, I go to the kitchen where my grandma is making breakfast. I make sure that I smile when I see her, I don't want her to see how upset I am because of that dream, I don't want her to worry about me. I love my grandma so much, but I feel as if I need to lie about these dreams because I don't want to disappoint her. She was Silver Dove when she was around my age and she fought hard, I bet she didn't have nightmares like I've been having. I know that she would never say it, but I think she would think I am being weak for being so afraid of the Crow. I can't help it though, I am scared about facing the Crow again. I've never really fought anyone before. I didn't really want to anyway. I've never wanted to fight anyone before, I love training in martial arts, but that is different. I just don't want to hurt anybody. Isn't that understandable?

When Grandma turns around and sees me enter the room, she smiles brightly at me and my bad dream is forgotten for the moment as she transfers some food from her frying pan to a few plates.

"Good morning Tesoro," Tesoro, her nickname for me. It means darling or treasure in Italian, "How did you sleep?" I smile at her and, not wanting to ruin her morning, I decide to lie.

"I slept well, how about you?"

"I slept well too." She brings me a plate of sunny-side-up eggs and toast. "Do you have any big plans for the day?" I shrug as I begin to nibble on my toast.

"Not much really, just school and martial arts practice afterward. Nothing really special, just a normal day." My grandma nods her head, suddenly solemn as she leans in closer to me, as if she wants to share a dirty little secret.

"Have you seen any sign of the Crow yet?" My grandma is the only one who knows that I am the one who fought against the Crow as my alter ego, Silver Dove. She is the one who gave me my powers in the form of a silver pin of a dove that I now have pinned to my cardigan. She used to be the Silver Dove before me while my grandfather was the Crow when they were younger. Now we can only guess who this new Crow is. I can only wonder how a magical pin can be used by this guy when they are only allowed to be used by people with good hearts. I can't even imagine what kind of goodness can be in a guy like him.

"No, not yet. It's been a few weeks now and nobody has seen a sign of him. It's almost as if he has disappeared off the face of the earth. You don't think he has given up, do you?" I ask this hopefully, but Grandma just returns my shrug.

"I don't know, but from the way you described him, I don't think the Crow is the kind of person who would quit on his mission. He will keep fighting until he has been defeated altogether or succeeds. We are both just going to have to keep trying to stop him until he sees the error of his ways." I look down at my breakfast, suddenly no longer hungry. That was exactly what I didn't want to hear.

As I start poking at my breakfast with my fork, trying to find my appetite, my dad comes into the kitchen, a big smile on his face as Grandma gets his breakfast ready. He gives me a kiss on the cheek as he sits down at his spot at the breakfast table.

"Good morning, my favorite ladies, how are you both this morning?" We both tell him that we're fine, quickly ending the serious conversation we were just having and starting a new one that is far more positive, hiding the subject of our original conversation.

My dad is an accountant in town and is the best dad a girl could ask for. My mom died when I was really young, so my dad asked my grandma to stay with us and help take care of me, and she has been with us ever since. Although our family isn't complete without my mom, I am still happy because I have been raised by two of the kindest people I have ever known. I feel as if I would be lost without the two of them. I consider them both my family, but I think of them as my best friends too. Dad is a great guy, but he doesn't know who I really am, Silver Dove. My dad would try to stop me if he did find out, but I still need to keep fighting against the Crow. I have to keep it a secret to make sure that everyone at school is safe from the Crow.

I finish my breakfast and kiss my grandma and dad goodbye as I head out my front door to wait for the bus at my mailbox. I'm ready, but not very eager, to start the day. We live outside of town, in the country, so it usually takes a while for the bus to show up. Leaning against the mailbox that has flowers painted on it, I pull out a book and start reading, trying to distract myself from the wait and the thoughts of my nightmare last night. I get about ten pages read before the bus finally pulls up. I hop on, eager to see my friends, yet scared of what might happen when I get to school in case the Crow does decide to come back to fight me. I have been having this feeling every time I get on the bus ever since the Crow first showed up and tried to scare everyone with those shadow dogs of his.

I sit down by myself until my best friend Natalie comes in on the bus's next stop. Natalie, or Nat as I call her, has been my best friend since Kindergarten, and I don't know how I could have gotten through my life without her, especially the past few weeks since the Crow showed up. She doesn't know who I really am, and I know that I can't tell her, but I wish I could. I wish I could have her support with this, but my grandma says that this must remain our secret. It hurts to keep such a major secret from my best friend, but I have to. As Silver Dove, I need to protect the people, not share my secrets with them. If I share that secret with one person it might leak out somehow and I will be putting myself in danger not only from the Crow, but from anybody else who wants to understand my powers and, possibly, steal them from me. I can't let that happen, so I must keep it a secret.

Nat is the kind of person that you want as a friend; she is kind, loyal, and always eager to have an adventure with you. Her intricate braids bounce against her back as she makes it to my seat and sits down beside me. Nat doesn't have many friends, she is a very shy person, but the people that she is friends with are very good people, and I am proud to say that she considers me to be her best friend, and she is mine.

We chat casually until the next stop and a boy walks on that we both recognize, Luis, a friend that we made the first day of class. Luis is a pretty tall guy, but he always seems to be hunched over as if he is afraid to show his true height, I suppose that is because he is shy like Nat. His dark hair always falls into his eyes, as if he is trying to hide his gaze from everyone. His shyness is almost painful to watch. I sometimes wonder if Nat and I are his only friends. Judging from the way he never seems to talk to anyone else, I wouldn't be surprised if we are. He is a very nice guy and he is fun to be around. I like him a lot, but Nat keeps telling me that she thinks he has a crush on me. I think she's just being silly, he is just a good friend, that's it.

As he smiles at me, I wonder what it would be like if he did have a crush on me, it would probably be hard for the both of us. Hard for him since he would have a crush on a girl that doesn't want to date anyone yet, and hard for me since I would still want to be friends with him but not his girlfriend. I don't want to date yet because I want to focus on school, I want to go to college and make my family proud. I want to be a doctor just like my mom was, but to do that, I need to work hard so that I can get as many scholarships as possible, so I can afford to go to college. Dating would only get in my way and distract me, so I will just have to wait before I start doing that. Luis sits on the seat in front of Nat and I, turning around so that he can face us.

"Good morning ladies, how are you?" I smile at him, forgetting those ideas of dating so that I can enjoy his company without feeling weird and awkward.

"I'm doing alright, how about you?" Luis smiles broadly at me.

"I'm doing fantastic." In that friendly smile, I can see why Nat would say he has a crush on me, but I know he's just being kind. Nat has always loved love stories. She just wants to see one acted out in real life for her.

"Did you hear about the two new clubs that some kids are trying to start up?" Nat asks us, her eagerness to tell us lighting up her eyes. She has always been the one who loves talking about the latest gossip. Luis and I both shake our heads. "Well a bunch of people are trying to start a fan club for Silver Dove-" I feel my heart soar with pride and joy, "as well as the Crow." And then my heart crashes back to earth.

"That sounds like it would be pretty cool club,"

Luis says enthusiastically, "Do you think you'll join the Crow's fan club Colomba?" I look to him to see if he is joking, but he looks completely serious. How can he ask me something like that? Does he think that I'm some kind of psycho?

"Of course not, why should I join the fan club of someone who destroys our school and threatens people with demonic shadow monster- things?" Luis looks a little hurt by what I said. Why is he hurt by what I said? It's probably because of the harsh tone I used. I force myself to calm down a bit before I speak again. "I'm sorry Luis, it's just that I can't believe anybody would want to make a club to support the Crow and what he's doing." Nat nods at this and explains it to me.

"Apparently, it's trying to be started by a lot of the bullied kids in school. They think of the Crow as their hero. He says that he will get rid of their bullies and they believe him. He gives them hope I guess." Nat says all of this and I am still horrified by it. How can he be a hero to anyone? Were those people not paying attention when the Crow was attacking everyone? Did they not see him act like a complete monster when he let all of those shadow monsters invade the school? Luis looks at me, the pained expression still on his face.

"Do you really think that badly of the Crow, Colomba?" I stare at him, at the misery in his eyes, and I realize that he is probably one of the Crow's supporters. Having one of his friends shame his hero must really hurt him. I bite my lip, trying to think of a way to explain myself in a kinder way, to not hurt my friend anymore.

"I'm sorry Luis. I just can't support anyone who hurts people to make a point, no matter how good the point may be. The Crow may have his followers, but I am not one of them, and I never will be as long as he hurts people." He nods his head, but I know that he doesn't agree with me. There is a darkness in his eyes, as if he is holding back a terrible rage that he doesn't want to direct at either me or Nat.

The rest of the bus ride to school is spent in silence between the three of us and I know that I am the one to blame for the awkwardness. I said something rude about someone Luis appears to look up to. Even though I don't think he should idolize the Crow, I should have said that in a much kinder way. I feel guilty about this, but I don't know what to say. The topic of the Crow and Silver Dove has become a really touchy subject at my school, and it seems to be an almost explosive topic with Luis and myself. I guess we are both being too passionate about this to be able to talk about it with each other.

When we finally make it to school, Luis separates from us to go to his first class while Nat and I stay together to head toward the class we share. As Nat and I sit down in our classroom, I look at her and ask for her advice, knowing that she is the perfect person to ask. She always seems to know what to do.

"Hey Nat, do you think I should say something to Luis? I think I upset him on the bus."

She shakes her head at me. "You already said you were sorry. You don't need to say it a billion times to get your point across. Besides he will forgive you and forget about it by lunch."

"Do you really think so?" I ask with hope welling up inside me.

"Of course, he could never stay mad at you forever."

I smile at my friend, knowing that she is telling the truth. I think that she is trying to imply that he "could never stay mad at me forever" since she thinks that he loves me, but I decide to ignore that. I don't want to bring that up and start an argument with her, I don't want to start two fights in one day. I have too much on my mind than to let myself add another argument to that long list of stuff I need to deal with.

The teacher walks into the classroom and begins the lesson. I give them my full attention, taking notes as they continue the lecture. I smile during the lesson, knowing that Nat is right. I can fix this with Luis, and I am sure that the fan club for the Crow will never be made. Silver Dove's fan club will probably get made, but not the Crow's.

The school would never support that. For now, I am safe.

Chapter Two

Luis-
My New Normal

As I sit down for my first class, my heart lies deep in my stomach. I can't believe that Colomba said something like that about me. Well she doesn't know that it is me. She said it about the Crow. If she did know that I am the Crow, would she have said those mean things? I can only hope that she wouldn't. I never want her to think badly of me.

Ever since school started, I have been in love with her. On our first day she stood up for me against one of my bullies, a bratty girl named Angela. She was brave and kind enough to do that for me even though we didn't know each other. Nobody has ever done anything like that for me before. As soon as I got my powers as the Crow with the Crow Medal that my uncle gave me, I decided that I was going to use my abilities to help other kids like me who are getting bullied at school. I am doing this to help them, and to also stop the people who are bullying me so that Colomba won't see me as someone weak. I can't let her see all of the people bullying me. If she does, then she might not want to be my friend anymore. I have had people stop being my friend because they saw how badly I was being bullied. They abandoned me so that they wouldn't get picked on too. I can understand why they did that, but it didn't take away the pain of them leaving.

As those painful memories run through my mind, I feel something bounce off the back of my head. Glancing down, I can see that it is a wad of crumpled up paper. Turning around, I see a guy named Alex high fiving one of his friends.

"Direct hit!" Alex laughs in triumph while I turn back around and lower my head, hoping that they will get bored and not do anything more to me. It doesn't take long for me to realize that my hopes were useless as several more paper wads hit me on my head and back while I just try and lose myself in my mind. This is a game they enjoy playing a lot. I have gotten used to it.

Alex has been my main bully since I was little. He used to be my best friend, but that didn't last long once people started picking on me. As soon as the bullying started he abandoned me and became the worst bully of all. The teacher, thankfully, walks in the room and starts class so Alex and his friend can no longer throw any more papers at me. I take notes, careful to not look up from my notebook in case Alex might try something if I look at him. He has done a lot of bad things to me before just because I looked at him. I don't want to tempt him today. I already feel bad enough with what happened with Colomba on the bus.

It feels like only minutes have passed when the bell rings, signaling the end of class. I pick up my books and papers and I try to quickly leave the classroom, but Alex beats me to the door and rams his shoulder into mine as he runs past me. I rub my shoulder as it throbs in pain while I walk down the hall to get to my next class. A small smile plays on my lips since I know that I will have my next class with Colomba. No matter how bad I am feeling, just knowing that I will see Colomba soon can make me feel a little better. That good feeling doesn't last very long when I see something that makes the blood in my veins turn into ice.

Walking down the hallway to her next class is Colomba. She is smiling up at Alex who is walking beside her, talking confidently with her like I wish I could. He says something that makes her laugh. It feels like someone has just stabbed me in the heart. It wasn't long after I met Colomba that I found out that Alex also knows her, and he seems to have feelings for her like me. Although we both have feelings for her, I doubt that he cares about her as much as I do, he probably only likes her because she is beautiful while I care about who she is as a person. I like listening to what she has to say while he probably isn't even listening to her right now.

As I watch them, all I can think is that maybe he is the one who will end up with her. He can talk to her without any fear and can make her laugh so easily. If he can do those things with ease maybe she would enjoy being with him. Would she want to be with him? If she does end up dating him would she never talk to me again and just forget I exist? Or would she join Alex in picking on me? I shake my head to get rid of that thought. Colomba is a sweet girl, she would never hurt anyone. To even think that she would is insulting to her.

Now that I have the Crow Medal, things might change for me. When I have gotten rid of all the bullies in school, then there won't be anyone in my way and I can be with Colomba without any fear. I smile as I think about that, one day I will reach that goal and I can finally walk down these school hallways without having to look over my shoulder all the time in case one of my bullies is following me. The only question is how am I going to do this?

When I saw Silver Dove a few weeks ago, she tried to convince me that this isn't the right way to end the bullying in our school. She seems to think that we should just let things go on as they are. She wants to let the bullies win and let all the innocent kids suffer in this school. Silver Dove is a moron, but she did give me a good idea though. Before I left her, she said that I can't fight the battles of the bullied kids for them. She was right about that, but she doesn't know that I can give them what they need to fight those battles. With the power of the Crow Medal I can summon shadow monsters that will do whatever I say, I can fly, and I can also give other people superpowers. I can give the bullied kids superpowers so that they can fight their own battles, they can get their revenge and teach the bullies not to mess with them. There is only one problem though. Who do I choose first?

There are a lot of students getting bullied at this school, but I don't know which one to choose. I need to choose the one who will understand why I have given them this power and use it in the right way. I need to find someone who can show the bullies exactly what they have been doing wrong. I need to make everyone so afraid to pick on each other that all the bullying will stop. Hopefully I can just transform this one person and that can make everyone see what they have been doing and change their ways. I don't want to fight this battle forever. I just want to do it once and get it over with. I need someone who will do as I say and not use their powers in the wrong way. I just need to be patient and find the right person. As I watch Colomba talk with Alex, I find it very hard to be patient.

Alex leaves her at the classroom door and walks off to his own class while I follow in after her and sit down at the desk beside her.

"Hey Colomba, how's it going?" She smiles at me and my heart beats faster just like it does every time she smiles at me.

"Everything is alright with me, how are you?" In complete honesty I am furious that Alex was speaking to her, but I won't say that to her. I'm not dating her, and it would be creepy to tell her that. It would make me sound jealous. I am jealous, but I don't want her to know that.

"Doing alright. I saw you talking to Alex Donner a second ago, are- are you friends with him?" I know it sounds like a strange question to ask someone, but I need to know what she thinks of him. I need to know if she likes him as more than friends. She thinks about my question for a moment before she answers.

"I suppose you could call him a friend. I met him on the first day of school in gym class and he was very nice to me. I haven't known him very long, but he seems like a good person."

"Well uh-" How do I say this without sounding like a complete jerk? "I don't think it would be a good idea for you to be around him-" The teacher suddenly comes in and starts class, not letting me finish my warning to Colomba. Before she starts taking her notes, she gazes at me curiously, obviously wondering what I was about to say about Alex.

The two of us take notes on what the teacher is saying about the Shakespeare play we are reading, but I am not really paying attention, I am trying to figure out how to warn Colomba about Alex without sounding like a terrible person. He has been acting nicely toward her ever since he met her because he thinks that she is pretty. Would she believe me if I told her that his kindness is a lie? Would she even want to believe me?

As I look over at her with her sweet, innocent eyes, I know that I have to protect her. I can't let someone like Alex hurt her in any way. No matter what he may do to me I need to warn Colomba about what a terrible person he is. I can't let him hurt her.

Chapter Three

Colomba-
The Tiger Girl

Stepping out of the classroom with Luis, we talk about the assignment the teacher just gave us for class. As he speaks, I think about what I said to him earlier about the Crow. He seemed so insulted by it. He is probably one of the people that Nat was talking about who likes what the Crow is doing. Although I don't understand why he would like someone like the Crow, I did apologize, but I still think that he is upset by what I said. Swallowing my fear, I speak up.

"Hey Luis?"

"Colomba, about Alex-" Luis says at the same time as I ask my question. We both chuckle before he says, "You go first."

"I'm sorry about what I said earlier on the bus about the Crow." He stares down at me, intrigued

by what I am saying. "I didn't mean to insult you."
He nods his head.

"It's okay."

"Can I ask why you support what the Crow is doing?" He looks down for a moment in thought before he answers me.

"Because he is doing what so many other people are too afraid to do. Everyone says you need to stop picking on other people, but nobody ever does anything to stop it. The Crow is finally putting an end to all of that so that everyone can come to school and be safe. Don't you think he should be respected for that?" He looks down at me with a hopeful glance, obviously wishing that I will agree with him. Sadly, I have to disappoint him.

"Anyone who tries to make peace and end suffering should be respected, but I think he is doing it in the wrong way. You can't scare someone into being a better person, it just doesn't work that way." He turns away from me looking crushed.

"Well, I think you might change your mind when the Crow starts changing this school for the better. Who knows, you might actually love him then." I shake my head.

"I don't think it will ever come to that. I'll talk to you later." I head into the gym for my next class while Luis watches me leave him, looking heartbroken. I want to make him feel better, but I know that the only way to do that is to agree with him and say that I like what the Crow says he will do. I can't do that. No matter how much I want him to feel better, I can't agree with him.

It only takes me a moment to get changed into my gym uniform and then I am back in the main room. I try to forget about what happened in the hallway with Luis so that I can focus on whatever we will be doing in class. It doesn't take long for a familiar voice to call out to me.

"Hello Gorgeous, how are you doing?" I turn around to see Alex walking toward me. A broad grin spread over his handsome face. I smile back at him, trying to be friendly.

"Hi Alex, I'm fine. How are you doing today?" He walks right up beside me, a little too close for my comfort, so I back away slightly.

"I'm doing fantastic as always. Can't be blue when I know that I get to see you every day." I try to smile at his words, but I can't make it a genuine smile. Alex has been very nice to me ever since I met him the first day of school, but sometimes he is just too nice. He also compliments me too much, it makes me a bit uncomfortable. I am not really used to having boys compliment me and flirt with me so openly. His confidence is almost intimidating sometimes. "Apparently, we are playing basketball today. We are pairing off to shoot baskets against each other. I already told the coach that we would be a pair, hope you don't mind." When he says that last part it feels as if he doesn't really care if I would have minded. He would have still made us partners anyway. I push that thought out of my mind though as he grabs us a ball and we start taking turns shooting the basket.

Basketball is actually one of my weaker sports, so Alex is easily beating me, especially since he is one of the star players on the basketball team. That is something that he likes showing off to me. Every time he makes a basket, he proudly states the score, obviously happy that he is beating me at something. Ever since we started this class together, he has always paired himself up with me and we are always either tied or I beat him in the sports. This is something that has always irritated him. Although he never says anything about it, I can see how much it frustrates him to know that a little girl like me can beat him. That is one thing about him that irritates me. He is very arrogant and loves to show off, but I don't want to push him away though since he is very kind to me, and it would be terrible of me to do that to someone when they are being kind. If he could just learn to think about somebody else for a change, then I might like being around him more.

While we continue to play, my mind wanders to my fight with the Crow. I had been absolutely terrified by everything that happened during the battle, but I still fought on despite all that. What scared me the most though is how the fight ended. I had tried to talk sense into the Crow, to tell him that this wasn't the right way to end the bullying in our school, but he wouldn't listen. I told him that he couldn't fight their battles for them. He thought about that for a moment and then admitted that I was right, but he had a way to help them fight their own battles. He left me after that while giving me a promise that he will return. I still don't understand what he meant by how he has a way for them to fight their own battles. How am I supposed to stop him if I don't even really understand what he is going to try and do?

As a superhero, I kinda feel like a complete failure. I didn't even really win the battle the last time, the Crow just left. Grandma believes in me though. She says that I will get the hang of my powers and I will defeat the Crow when he does come back. I only wish that I had her confidence. I have a sickening feeling in my stomach that tells me that I will lose. I can't defeat someone as powerful as him. This fight is impossible for me. I might as well give up.

The class passes by quickly and Alex defeats me completely, winning all five games we played together. By the end of class I am just happy that it's over. I don't think I could have stood another minute listening to Alex proudly proclaiming the score. I would have probably lost it and either quit or tell Alex to stop showing off, it's annoying. I know it would have been mean, but *man* was he being annoying.

As soon as I have gotten myself cleaned up and back into my normal clothes, I rush out of the gym before Alex can find me again to start talking and I start walking to my next class. I actually find myself releasing a sigh of relief now that I am out of Alex's company. The hallway is bustling with people as they head to their next class as well. While I watch people talking with their friends and laughing happily. I try to find the evidence of the bullying that the Crow was telling me about, but I don't see anything bad. People are smiling and having a good day; where is the bullying? Maybe I am just naïve, and I think too highly of people. I think that everything is alright when it is actually terrible for a lot of other people. Nat joins me as I walk and she starts telling me about a funny story she had heard in her last class, but my mind still focuses on that question. Where is the bullying the Crow was talking about?

My thoughts are interrupted as I jump slightly when I hear something crashing to the ground. Turning around, I see a girl picking herself up from the floor so that she can stand on her hands and knees to pick up some books and papers that she had dropped while several people laugh at her as they walk past, not even bothering to help her. She is a small girl, probably a freshman like me with mousy brown hair and large, fearful eyes that scan everyone who passes her as if she is afraid of them. Her tiny body is covered by a large hooded sweatshirt. The hood is up, which almost completely hides her face. The parts of her face that aren't hidden by her hood are nearly covered by her hair which is falling in her face. The girl quickly gathers her papers in a frantic heap in her hands as everyone steps over her as if they don't even realize that she exists.

Rushing over to her, I go down on my knees so that I can help her pick up her remaining papers. When she sees me, she stops what she is doing for a moment and stares at me, as if she can't believe that someone is helping her. She's looking at me as if I am some kind of hallucination that only she can see. She looks down and continues to pick up her papers when I look up and smile at her. Clearing my throat, I try to start a conversation.

"I'm sorry that happened. Did you hurt yourself when you fell?" She shakes her head quickly, her eyes darting back and forth as if she's afraid that I am just distracting her so that somebody else can sneak up behind her.

"No, I- I'm fine." A soft voice says from beneath the hood. She picks up her papers and books as quickly as she can, as if she is trying to get away from me as fast as possible. As I pick up another book, I notice something coming out from between the pages. Opening the book, I see that it is a photograph. In the photo stands the girl in front of me with an older man, who I am guessing to be her father, standing in our town's small zoo. What really catches my eye about this picture though is that they are both holding tiger cubs. The tiger cubs look to be only a few days old, their fur is only just starting to appear, and their little eyes look at the camera with curiosity. They don't seem to be scared about being in the hands of some random human. It's as if they trust the girl in front of me and her father, as if those tigers love them.

"Do you work at the zoo?" She glances up at me in surprise, revealing a pair of beautiful green eyes.

"Yeah, how did you know?" I hold up the picture to show her. "Oh, right. I work with my dad to take care of the tigers." I smile brightly at her, completely fascinated by this girl. She is brave enough to handle tigers, but she is afraid of talking to a regular person. This girl is confusing.

"That's amazing!" She smiles timidly. "I wish I could do something like that. It must be amazing to do something that awesome and get paid for it." I pick up her last paper and we both stand up. She holds all of her disorganized papers and books tightly in front of her chest, casting her eyes to the ground.

"Thanks."

"No problem, it was nice talking to you. I'll try and find you next time I go to the zoo. I would love to talk with you again." She nods quickly before practically running away from me.

"What was that all about?" Nat asks me, I shrug my shoulders.

"I don't know, I suppose she's just shy." Nat shakes her head at me.

"Birdy, I am shy, she is beyond that. She is paralyzed by people." The two of us continue to walk to class as I watch the tiger girl practically running ahead of us to get away.

People snicker and grin at her as she goes past them. One guy even purposefully sticks his leg out so that she stumbles over it, almost falling to the ground again. The snickering starts again when everyone sees her stagger, as if that is somehow funny. How could watching someone getting picked on be funny? Why are they picking on her? Is it because she is so shy that she just ran away from me to avoid talking to me?

From what I can guess, this girl has been getting picked on for a long time. When I spoke to her she seemed surprised that I was speaking to her in a friendly way. As if she expected me to insult her instead of helping her pick up her books. That person who tried to trip her, and the people who laughed at her, have probably been picking on her for years. The only reason I don't know this is because I went to a different school than most of the people here. I went to a small private school, Doyle Academy, while most of the other people in my class went to the local middle school. Because of this, I have had to meet a lot of new people and learn a lot of things about them to understand a lot of what they talk about. One thing I am glad I didn't know about from the local middle school is all of the bullying. I don't want to know why these other people are getting picked on by my classmates. I just want to help end it. I never want to see anyone as afraid of another person as that girl was with me just now.

As Nat and I continue walking, I realize something. I think I finally have an answer to the question I was thinking of only moments before, this is where the bullying is.

Chapter Four

Luis-
The Drawing

Fourth period, one of my favorite classes, art. I am always the first to arrive and the last to leave. As soon as I sit down, I am working on one of our assignments. This month we are focusing on drawing animals, and this week we are working on birds. Our teacher let us choose our own birds to draw for the project. It wasn't very surprising, with everything that has been going on, to find out that everyone is drawing either a dove or a crow. From what I can see, whichever one they chose is the person they support the most. I'm not surprised that when Alex showed everyone his drawing in class yesterday it was a dove, and not a very well-drawn dove at that. I don't think in a million years Alex would ever support me as the Crow. I'm here to get rid of all the bullying in this school and he's one of the biggest ones. When I make him stop bullying, I will be getting rid of his favorite hobby. Naturally he would support Silver Dove who wants to keep everything as it is. I can't stand her.

Looking down at my sketchbook, I admire my drawing. It is of a crow flying through the air. Its beak is open wide as it lets out a cry and its talons pointing out, as if it is about to fight someone. It is a very good drawing, even the teacher, Mr. Sizemore, said that it was fantastic. I start working on adding details on the feathers of the wings as everyone else files in. I am grateful that Mr. Sizemore walks in before Alex so that he doesn't have the opportunity to do anything to me while the teacher is not around. As soon as everyone is seated, Mr. Sizemore tells everyone to get to work on their drawings and then proceeds to walk around the room to help anyone who needs assistance. When he stops by me, he glances down at my drawing and smiles at it.

"That is an impressive bird you have there." I smile up at him.

"Thanks Mr. Sizemore."

"It's well deserved, everyone seems to be drawing a dove or a crow this week. Interesting how that turned out." He says the last part of that statement sarcastically since we both know why everyone is drawing those two birds.

"Hey Mr. Sizemore." He looks at me curiously,

hearing the discomfort in my voice.

"Yes?"

"Who do you think is the good guy with all this, the Crow or Silver Dove?" He silently stares down at my drawing, thinking about my question. An entire minute passes in silence before he gives me an answer.

"I think that the two of them believe that they are fighting for the right reasons. I can't say for certain which one is right or not. The Crow may have wrecked the school, but he seems to have a reason for fighting. He seems to be someone in pain while Silver Dove comes in and tries to fight him, also saying that she is fighting for the right reasons. I can't pass judgement on someone when they are trying to do what is right, even if they may do things in the wrong way." He gives me a small smile as he leaves me to help a girl sitting behind me who is having trouble drawing the beak of her bird. Well that was a cop out answer.

Staring down at my drawing again, I think about what he said. So far, he is the only teacher that hasn't condemned me as the Crow for what I did. All the other teachers have been complaining and persecuting me for what happened. They all say that I have to be some kind of monster for doing what I did. Don't they notice what all of the other kids are doing to the bullied kids like me? If they did notice then they would say that I am the good guy, saving all of the poor kids who can't defend themselves. I think that Mr. Sizemore is the best teacher I have ever had.

The bell rings, ending the class much too soon in my opinion. I walk out to head to my next class. I miraculously make it there without anyone tripping me or something and class begins like normal. After a few minutes though I excuse myself to head to the bathroom. As I wash my hands, I glance around to make sure that nobody else is inside before I open up my jacket where I have hidden my Crow Medal. Placing my hand on top of it, I hear a sudden rush of wind and a large crow appears on top of a paper towel dispenser.

"Hi Shadow."

"Hello Master." The crow responds to me in a friendly voice. Ever since I got this medal, she has been with me whenever I need her. Most of the time I just want to talk to her though. I've been telling her about my idea of giving one of the bullied kids powers and she listens to me. As I look up at her, I ask her something that I have been wondering about for a while now but have been too afraid to ask.

"Shadow, can I ask you something?"

"Of course, Master, you can ask me anything you want." I stare down at my hands as I wash them.

"Do you approve of my plan to help get rid of the bullies?" She looks away from me and stares down at her talons, taking a moment to think.

"I am merely your guide, I am not here to tell you what to do. I am here to help you reach your goal. I came to you because I could see that you have a good heart. I know that no matter what, you will always do what you think is right and you will come out victorious in the end." Well that was a bit of a cop out answer too I think to myself, but I don't dare to say that out loud.

"Thanks Shadow, it's just that everyone is taking sides on who they support, me or Silver Dove, and it is nice to know that at least you are on my side." She nods at me, her black eyes evaluating me.

"You're upset that Colomba does not approve of your actions?" Now it is my turn to nod at her uncomfortably.

"Yeah, I'm doing all of this for her. I want our school to be a better place, and she won't see me as a pathetic kid who gets picked on all the time. It's horrible to think that she thinks the Crow is the bad guy. What do you think about this? Do you think she'll change her mind?" Shadow shrugs her wings at me.

"I do not know. I'm not in her mind like I am in yours." I feel my eyes grow wide in terror.

"Wait, you're in my mind?! You can hear my thoughts!?" Shadow chuckles.

"Yes, only sometimes though. Your thoughts

are very interesting."

"Shadow, I-" I hear someone opening the door to the bathroom. Placing my hand over the medal again, Shadow disappears. Lowering my head, I leave the bathroom quickly so that whoever is coming in won't have the opportunity to try anything on me. The bathroom is one of the places that my bullies like cornering me in. Rushing past whoever it is, I walk back to class, hoping that the rest of the day will go by quickly and that Shadow isn't spying on my thoughts again.

I return to class, sitting down to finish up my assignment, boredom making my eyes heavy while my mouth opens up into a huge yawn. I'm not sure about the second wish I made in the hallway, but the first one does come true. The rest of the day passes quickly and in no time, I am on the bus heading home. Colomba, Nat, and I talk, but not as happily as we normally do. I suppose we all still feel pretty awkward about our disagreement this morning. I make it to my uncle's antique shop without a problem. Since he is talking with a customer, I head straight up the stairs into our apartment on the second floor and flop down on my bed in my room, exhausted after such a long day.

Softly, I can hear Uncle Diego chatting with the customer in the shop. In the silence of my room, I wonder what he would do if he found out that I am the Crow. He was so upset after that first time I appeared as the Crow. He just kept condemning me for what I did at the school. He only seemed upset because he was afraid that I was going to hurt someone. Would he feel better if he knew that I don't plan on hurting anybody? I just want to teach the bullies a lesson. Would he make me end my mission even if he knew that?

I can't tell him who I am, I know he wouldn't like me if he knew the real me. He loves me as his nephew, but he would hate me as the Crow. I get up off my bed and walk over to my desk. Taking out a sheet of paper from the top drawer, I examine it carefully. Written on it neatly is a long list of names. I think about each name with caution because I know what these names are meant for. This is my list of possible people who will become the first soldier in my cause, a list of all the bullied kids.

Chapter Five

Colomba-
Practice

Using all of my concentration, I swing the katana down and strike through my target. It is after the usual martial arts class and my teacher, Jeff, is giving me extra private lessons. Right now, we are doing a practice with the katana, or Japanese sword, where you are to slice through a tatami, or grass mat, that has been rolled up with your katana to try and get the sword to slice all the way through it smoothly. Whenever an expert does it, it looks easy, but it most definitely is not, especially if you want to do it correctly. Placing my sword back in its sheath, Jeff examines the cut I had made on the rolled-up mat. He nods as he scrutinizes it.

"Very nice, but look here," he points to the center of the rolled-up mat, "you scalloped there a little bit." I sigh softly. When he says scalloped, it means that my cut curved too much when it should have been straight. He notices my frustration since he smiles at me. "It's okay though, we have been going at this for over an hour. We can try again another day. You look exhausted." I smile at him gratefully.

"Thanks, I am pretty beat." The two of us sit down on the floor as we clean the blades. That's something you should always do after using a sword. After that we start sweeping up the cut-up bits of mat that have spread out across the floor.

Jeff has been teaching me martial arts for years now. He has almost been like an uncle to me. Recently, he has also been a major help as I have taken on my role of Silver Dove even though he doesn't know it. Whenever I transform into Silver Dove I have a sword on me. Jeff has been helping me learn how to use swords better so that I can fight with it more effectively whenever the Crow decides to pop back up again. I wish I could tell him who I really am and tell him how much he has helped me, but I can't. Only Grandma and I must know that. If I want to keep everyone safe, I must stand alone. I suppose my new superpowers can be both a blessing and a curse. I am now able to do all these awesome things like fly and have super strength, but I also can't really share that with any of my friends. I can't tell them without putting a huge target on their backs and have someone like the

Crow hurt them. I would rather harm myself than to have someone I love to be harmed. I sometimes feel as if I am alone in this world now that I have this pin and being alone is one of the worst feelings anybody can experience.

It doesn't take us long to finish cleaning the swords and sweeping the floor. We put up the brooms just as my grandmother pulls the car in the back-parking lot to pick me up. As I open the door to leave, Jeff calls out to me.

"Hey Colomba!" I turn back to look at him.

"Yes?"

"Have you guys heard anything more about the Crow or Silver Dove? Has anybody seen a sign of them?" I shake my head at him.

"Nope, nothing." I lie, wanting nothing more than to tell him the truth.

"When they do show up again, make sure you pay attention to Silver Dove's sword work. From what I saw from the clip they keep showing on the news, she is very good with it and you can learn a thing or two from observing her." I smile to myself, feeling proud of his compliment.

"Alright, I will." I close the door behind me and get in the car. I smile at my grandma, feeling ten feet tall after Jeff's compliment.

"How was practice Tesoro?"

"It was great, we practiced how to cut properly. It's definitely going to come in handy when the

Crow comes back." Grandma smiles softly to herself.

"I remember what it was like practicing with my powers when I had the pin. When I met your grandfather and we found out that we both had these magical pins, we would practice together." She chuckles, "I remember this one time, not too long after we met, we were practicing together, and he wanted to show off to me. He decided to fly high into the air and do some tricks, but he accidently flew into an eagle, who was not very happy about being flown into. The eagle chased him for miles and when he came back to me, he was covered in feathers, dirt, and hay. Apparently to try and get away from the eagle he tried to fly through a barnyard and accidently crashed into a barn. He had to fly away again because then he was being chased by the eagle *and* the farmer who owned the barn. It took him almost an hour to get them both off his trail before he came back to me." We both laugh at the story, the two of us remembering a sweet man that we both miss dearly.

When we arrive at home, my grandmother, father, and I all gather for dinner and enjoy a good meal before I go up to my room and finish my homework before getting into bed, but sleep does not come to me. Picking myself up out of bed, I walk over to my window and look outside. It is completely dark; the only light present comes from the half-moon that hangs in the sky above me. Knowing that sleep won't come for me for a while, I decide that the best way to wear myself out is to go out and fly around for a little bit. Glancing at my alarm clock on my bedside table I can see that it isn't too late, so I don't feel too bad as I put my pin on my pajamas. I place my hand over it and say the magic words, "Peaceful warrior." Instantly I transform into Silver Dove. Smiling to myself, I open my window and leap outside, letting my wings spread out wide as I take flight.

At first, I pay careful attention to what I am doing, since flying is still something new to me, but as I get more comfortable, I let my mind wander as the tranquility of the night radiates around me. I see dark windows in the homes of sleeping people, lonely cars heading home from a long day of work, and the animals of the night heading out of their dens. I think that it is far more relaxing to fly at night than it is to fly during the day. I don't have to worry about having other people seeing me, and I don't have to worry about as many birds to fly into like my grandfather did all those years ago.

As I fly through the air, I smile peacefully, enjoying the feeling of the wind in my face. Everything feels perfect for a moment, a moment that is suddenly ruined when something flies into my face. I let out a shriek of terror as I fly frantically, trying to pull whatever it is off my face.

"Oh my gosh! Get it off! I can't see! I can't see!" I finally claw it off to reveal a piece of newspaper. When I look ahead to see where I am going, I see that I am flying straight into the side of a building. I feel my heart stop. "I don't want to see." I don't even have time to stop or even cover my face before I fly face first into the brick building and then fall to the ground, letting out a low moan. Taking in a deep breath, I pause for a moment as I thank my lucky stars. "Thank you for invincibility." Crushing the newspaper in my hand and tossing it into a nearby trashcan. I pick myself up and shake my wings, getting the dirt and leaves out from between my feathers. "Why is it that every time I try to go out for a nice flight around town, I have to hit something with my face?" I laugh to myself as I think about how similar what just happened is to my grandmother's story. Apparently, my grandfather and I are very similar with our powers, we both are terrible fliers.

I spread out my wings, stretching them after my impact. Looking back at them, I smile. I think that my wings are one of my favorite parts about my powers. I may not be a good flier, but it doesn't mean that I don't enjoy it. I love flying around whenever I have the chance and I just love how majestic I look with these wings. They are huge and covered in long white feathers. With my wings and silver armor on, I almost look like a warrior angel.

From what people have been saying about me on the news that is how a lot of people view me as well. I am the angel who is saving them from the monster called the Crow. I suppose, if I am an angel, then in everyone's minds the Crow must be a demon. He sort of fits that description with his dark costume and black wings, but something in the back of my mind is telling me that he isn't a bad person on the inside. He wants people to be happy, he is just doing it in a terrible way. That is at least what my grandma has been saying, but I think she always sees the best in people. I try to do that, and I am usually successful at it, but with the Crow, all I can really see is darkness. I have a feeling deep in my chest that my war with him will take a very long time and I can only hope that I will come out the victor in the end.

I shake my head, trying to get those morbid thoughts out of my mind before I open my wings again and take off into the air. Flying through the night sky, I head back home. Paying attention to where I am going this time, so I won't fly into any more buildings. I'm not sure if I will fall asleep now despite my flight around town. Even though I have worn out my body, my mind is now racing with thoughts of the Crow. I will probably have another nightmare tonight. I release a sigh, knowing that I will be exhausted tomorrow.

Chapter Six

Luis-
The First One

As I sit on the bus and look back at Colomba in the seat behind me I am instantly concerned. Her eyes are dull, lacking their usual sparkle, and she doesn't have her normal smile on her face. Dark circles haunt underneath her eyes

"Is anything wrong Colomba?" She smiles up at me weakly, as if she is trying to put on a brave face to make sure I won't worry about her.

"No, I'm just really tired. I couldn't get to sleep last night."

"Really, what was keeping you up?" She shrugs her shoulders as if it doesn't really matter.

"Just a lot on my mind I suppose. I even went out for a... run, but that didn't even help."

"Maybe you should just try counting sheep to help you go to sleep. That's what I do." Natalie chimes in.

"Whenever I can't sleep I just-" I stop myself before I can say it. I could kick myself right now. I have never told anyone about that, and I wasn't planning to, but I guess I'm just so comfortable around these two that it almost slipped out. Natalie noticed my sudden stop since she eyes me carefully as she asks me a question.

"What were you saying that you do Luis?" Lowering my gaze from them, I answer honestly, knowing that they would recognize whether I was lying or not.

"When I can't go to sleep, I dance." This seems to wake Colomba up since her eyes grow wide and she smiles wide at me.

"You dance?" I can feel my face growing warm and I know that I am blushing furiously. I lower my head, not wanting either of them to see me blush.

"Yeah, before my parents died, they used to be dance teachers. Whenever I can't sleep, I do some of the dance steps that they and my uncle taught me. I was really young when they died, but that is one of the things I really remember about them."

"That's so sweet." I look up to see that Colomba is smiling sweetly, in no way teasing me. "Whenever I get frustrated, I think of some of the songs my grandfather taught me from Italy to make me feel better. I think of it as a wonderful way to keep him alive. I guess that's what you can say for your dancing with your parents." I am actually stunned by her words, I thought that she would laugh at me for that, but she actually thinks of it in a good way. She even said it was sweet. I find myself blushing again, but not out of embarrassment.

We spend the rest of the bus ride talking about the different kinds of dances that my parents taught me. When we do get to school, we separate to go to our own classes where I have to hide my happiness, so Alex won't notice it and try to ruin it for me. I didn't get to warn Colomba about Alex since we started arguing again, but I know that I will need to do it soon. He keeps getting closer to her, and that is dangerous, he will hurt her. I just know it. I know I can't tell her now though since she probably wouldn't listen. She is already pretty mad at me and would think that I am just trying to make her upset at somebody else instead of me if I did tell her about Alex.

Once I finish the assignment that the teacher assigned us, I get permission to go to the bathroom. Sitting on top of the sink counter, I place my hand over the Crow Medal so that Shadow can appear beside me on the counter.

"Hello Master. What can I do for you?"

"I was just wondering if you can answer a question for me." She nods her head.

"Of course, I can."

"Well you told me that you can sometimes hear my thoughts, what exactly have you heard?" She chuckles softly, a little mischievously.

"I've heard you talk about how much you hate your biology class, thinking about how to make some extra money, and, oh right, I've also heard what you think about Colomba." She makes kissing sounds at me as she laughs teasingly. Turning on the sink faucet, I splash water at Shadow. She fluffs out her feathers as she shakes herself, trying to get the water off, still laughing.

"You're terrible." I say as I smile to her, accepting her teasing. A sudden thought comes to me. I look at Shadow, suddenly curious. "How did you make that kissing sound without lips?" She chuckles again as she holds her head high, her beak pointing up in the air.

"Talent." I can't help but laugh again.

"You're such a dork."

"Thank you." She states with pride.

Suddenly, I hear someone coming into the bathroom. Looking at the door, I see it opening. Thinking quickly, I grab Shadow and hide her in my jacket. She squawks loudly for only a moment in her shock until she also hears the person walk in. A guy I recognize from my biology class walks in and stares at me curiously.

"What was that?" I stare at him, pretending not to know what he is talking about.

"What was what?" He scoffs at me.

"You know what I'm talking about freak, that weird shrieking sound. You must have heard it too. It sounded like it was coming from in here." I shake my head at him.

"Sorry, I didn't hear a thing." I walk past him, still holding Shadow beneath my jacket. Only once we are safely in the hallway do I hear Shadow's voice softly whispering from beneath my jacket.

"You could have just put your hand on the medal, and I would have flown back into it you know?"

"I couldn't" I whisper back to her, "he was too close and that takes a few seconds to do. He would have seen us doing it and would have asked too many questions."

"Oh, and shoving me in your jacket didn't cause him to ask a question or two?" I have to take a deep breath to not make myself lose my temper.

"Well if you didn't squawk so loudly, he may not have asked any questions at all. Ow!" I remove my hand from my jacket, shaking it in my pain. Looking down at my hand, I can see a red mark that, even though it didn't break the skin, still hurts. In an instant I know what happened, Shadow pecked me. "Oh, that was really mature." I grumble under my breath. Shadow definitely heard it though since I feel her peck me again on my chest. "Ow! Come on Shadow, just wait a moment to let me see whether or not anybody else is in the hallway, then I will put you back in the medal. Okay?" She doesn't say anything, so I assume she agrees with me. I glance down the hallway and I don't see anyone. When I look around a corner though to see an adjacent hallway, I find two other people.

The only one I recognize is a girl named Angela, a snobby brat of a girl who thinks she's better than everyone else and enjoys picking on anyone she can. The way I was introduced to her was that on the first day of school, I tripped over her purse and she started yelling at me. That is also how I met Colomba, she got in between Angela and I and got her to stop yelling at me. She defended me. I smile at the memory, almost glad that I met a horrible girl like Angela, because she helped me get introduced to the greatest person I have ever met. Angela has long blonde hair and is incredibly thin, she is actually so thin that she can easily be compared to a child's stick figure drawing.

She is walking toward the other person, who I don't recognize. I can't even see their face because their face is almost completely covered by a hood they are wearing. I ask myself how they can see where they are going since they are looking down at the ground as they walk, but that question is quickly answered, they can't. As they pass by Angela they bump into her, a big mistake. Angela turns to face them, rage igniting her eyes.

"How dare you do that! Who do you think you are?!" The person with the hood turns to face her and I finally see their face. She is a small girl, probably a freshman like me, with brown hair and huge, frightened eyes. Truthfully, I can understand her fear. If I was confronted by Angela again, I would be terrified too. The girl is practically quivering in fear as Angela glares down at her while she averts her gaze from hers.

"I'm really sorry." The girl whispers, her voice shaking in her terror.

"*Sorry?* You should be sorry you little freak. Don't ever come near me. I don't want to see your pathetic face again." Angela stalks off, leaving the terrified girl cowering against some lockers, staring after her in terror before running off in her fear like a frightened rabbit. As the two of them disappear from my sight, I find myself smiling at what just happened.

"Did you see that Shadow?"

"Yes, I did. I feel so sorry for that poor girl."

"Me too, and I think I know how to make her feel better. I'll forget about my list for right now, I think I found my first soldier."

Chapter Seven

Colomba-
The Tiger Girl's
Pain

Walking through the school hallways I keep my eyes peeled for the tiger girl that I met yesterday. Something in the back of my mind tells me that I need to look out for her. She is the kind of person that the Crow says he is trying to save from the bullies in our school, but I don't want him to influence her in any way. The Crow may want to "save her", but I want to help her.

It doesn't take me long to find her, it's surprisingly easy to find a person who is getting picked on, at least if you pay attention. She is trying to walk down the hallway peacefully, but a group of boys are following her, throwing things at the back of her hooded head and saying rude things to her. From where I am, I can hear one of them telling her to look at him. The tiger girl doesn't do what he says, not to defy him, but because she is afraid to. She is afraid to look at him. The boy seems to realize this since he laughs in her face while she tries to run away from them through the hallway but can't get very far considering how crowded it is.

Squirming my way through the crowd, I make it to her side and wrap my arm around her shoulder. She flinches at my touch, but I don't pay attention to that. I look behind us to see that the boys are walking away now. They aren't interested in her anymore now that they can see that she isn't alone. I smile at her, trying to comfort her in her time of need.

"Hi, how are you today?" I know that she probably isn't doing too well considering what just happened, but I need to get a conversation going so that if the boys try and come back to pick on her again, they can see that I haven't left her. She doesn't look at me, and I feel her body stiffen under my arm. I can see that she is terrified that I am talking to her, but I need to keep talking to her to make sure that nothing happens and to show her that I have her back. I may only be one person but having at least one person on your side is better than having nobody.

"I'm okay." She manages to whisper beneath her hood, which she is hiding her face from me with. I smile at her, but she doesn't return my smile.

"That's good, where are you heading?" Her hands tighten around the books she is holding in her hands.

"English."

"Well that's great, my class is around the English wing. Mind if I walk with you?" That is actually a complete lie. My next class is practically on the other side of the school, but I want to talk with her, I want to get to know her. She, on the other hand, does not seem interested in getting to know me.

"I- I've got to go." She stutters before she runs away from me down the hall, trying to get away as fast as possible. Nat was right, she isn't just shy, she is paralyzed by people. I have never met anybody who is as afraid of people as her.

As I watch her go, it feels as if my heart is being crushed in my chest. How can I complete my mission to help this girl if she doesn't even want my help?! Can't she see that I want to be her friend and get the bullies to stop picking on her?! I feel like screaming right now in frustration, it's like I've been given an impossible job to do yet I'm still expected to complete it. What am I going to do? If I can't help even one bullied kid how am I supposed to help all the others before the Crow tries to do something terrible again?

Turning away from the tiger girl's retreating figure, I hurry to my own class, running through the halls even though I know I'm not supposed to. I make it into the classroom just as the bell is ringing and I take my seat, my heart pounding in my chest from the run. As the teacher starts talking, I take notes, but my mind is really focused on that tiger girl. What do I need to do to help her? What can I possibly do to help a girl who is so shy that she runs away from people? How can I possibly convince her that I want to be her friend and I want to help her get out of her shell so that she doesn't have to be afraid of the world?

I try to push that girl out of my mind so that I can focus on class, but the lesson just doesn't sink in. My hand scribbles down notes, but I don't pay attention to what I write. What am I going to do?

Chapter Eight

Luis-
Finding Evidence

From behind a corner, I watch as several boys throw things at the girl that I hope will become my first soldier. Even though the boys are throwing things at her and saying rude things she just keeps walking, trying to hide her face beneath that hood of hers. I know what she's going through right now. I've had this happen to me many times. She is trying to ignore them, hoping that they will just get bored and walk away to find someone else to pick on. She is so afraid right now, but those guys don't show her any mercy. It's almost as if they don't think of her as a human being. As if they are better than her.

When I start thinking that there is no hope for her, someone actually steps forward and helps her. The person goes up to her and wraps their arm around her shoulders as if they are best friends and starts talking to her. As soon as the boys see that the girl isn't alone, they walk away, probably to go torture somebody else. I smile when I see who is the one that has come to this poor girl's rescue, Colomba.

Is this how she meets everyone in this school, defending them from some bully? I mean, that's how we met. It was at that moment that she became one of the only true friends I have ever had. When I think about it, she is probably the only true friend I've ever had. Wow I just depressed myself with that thought.

Colomba tries to talk to the bullied girl, but it doesn't take long before the girl runs away from her, too terrified to speak to her. Wow, if she's scared about talking to someone as nice as Colomba then she must be really scared of people.

I have seen this girl before, she used to go to my old middle school. I never talked to her, but I have seen her getting picked on a lot. From what I have heard, she has always been like this, running away from people like how most people run away from spiders. This girl is everything you would expect from a bullied kid; she lets everyone pick on her. I don't think she has any friends, and she never really talks to anyone. I'm surprised Colomba could get her to say three words, that's almost a miracle. I've gone to school with that girl for years and I don't think I've heard her say anything.

The reason I've been watching her is because I need to know whether or not I should make her my first soldier. I can give her the powers to fight back against her bullies, but I want to be sure that she is going to use her powers right and do what I say. I have a mission and I won't let anyone get in the way of that. After what I have just seen I'm starting to believe that I may have been right, this girl may be the one I need to come back as the Crow again and show all the mean kids that they can't mess with the kids like me anymore. I won't let them.

I stare at Colomba as she watches the bullied girl run away. She is so beautiful. Even now that she is upset because this girl has run away from her, she is still beautiful. I want to go over to her and tell her that everything will be alright. I want to, but I know I can't. If I did that, then it would show her that I have been spying on her and that other girl. That would be a little creepy by most people's standards and I never want to look creepy to her. So instead of comforting the girl of my dreams, I have to stand back and watch as her face falls before she runs in the opposite direction, heading to class.

I head to my class as well, my hands clenched into fists at my sides. No matter what I want to end the bullying at this school, but I also want to make sure that Colomba never has to see someone get picked on like that again. I could easily see how much it upset her to see that girl go through that. Colomba is the kind of person who feels like she needs to help those in trouble, but I don't want her to have to do that again because I know that it hurts her so much to see people in pain. I also never want her to see me getting picked on. I don't want her to look at me the way she did as she was watching that girl run away. In her eyes I could see her pitying that girl. I never want her to pity me. I would hate myself if she ever looked at me like that.

I make it to class with a few minutes to spare before the teacher starts the lesson, so I pull out my sketchbook and start working on a few doodles. All around me people are talking, laughing, and enjoying each other's company while I am all alone. Being lost in the crowd, it is an art that I have mastered through years of painful practice.

Chapter Nine

Colomba-
Jeje

When school ends everyone rushes through the front doors, either heading for a bus or to one of the waiting cars driven by impatient parents. While everyone else is eagerly trying to reach their ride home, I scan through the crowd, trying to find the girl I had met earlier, the tiger girl. I just know that something bad will happen involving her. My grandma told me, when she gave me the Dove Pin, that I will start developing a third sense that will tell me when something bad is about to happen, something that will need Silver Dove's help to fix. I think I have that feeling now involving that girl, I need to help her before whatever it is happens.

The Crow said that he is going to "help" the

bullied kids in our school. Judging from what I have seen from that girl she might be the perfect target for the Crow. I need to show her now that she does not need help from the Crow, that she is not alone in this school. She can have a friend. I can be that friend to her.

Looking through the crowd I can't spot her among the endless sea of people. One person, apparently, doesn't have any trouble finding me though.

"Hello Beautiful, how's it going?" I glance over my shoulder to see Alex walking over to me with his usual, confident smile on his handsome face.

"Hey Alex." I start looking around again, trying to find the girl. He walks up beside me. He's standing a bit too close for my taste, so I move slightly to the side. Alex easily notices that I am not paying attention to him, so he asks me a question.

"What are you looking for?"

"I'm looking for a girl I met earlier; she's kinda small and has brown hair. She apparently works at the zoo." Alex chuckles at me and I stop my search through the crowd to stare at him curiously, not really understanding why he is laughing.

"What's so funny?" He looks at me as if I am being silly.

"I know who you're talking about, but why

would you want to look for her? She's a complete freak." I feel myself recoil slightly at his harsh tone.

"Alex, you should never say that about anyone." He looks away and bites his lower lip softly, something I see him do often. He does it whenever he realizes that he has said something that upsets me and is trying to think of a way to make up for it or explain himself. He says a lot of stuff that upsets me, so I see him do it a lot. I know that he doesn't like upsetting me, but he talks about other people quite a bit and it usually isn't nice.

"I'm sorry Colomba, but what else would you call a girl who runs away when anyone tries to talk to her? You have to admit that's a bit weird." I turn away from him, annoyed.

"You can't blame someone for being shy. That just means you need to show them kindness to help them understand that they are welcome." He doesn't say anything to that, it looks as if he wants to disagree with me but doesn't want to upset me further. From the corner of my eye I see a familiar hooded sweatshirt. "I'll see you later Alex, I've found her." I walk away from him, trying to let my annoyance disappear as I walk toward the tiger girl who is standing underneath a tall oak tree by herself. She's holding her books close to her chest as if she is afraid that somebody will try and knock them out of her hands. Truthfully, I wouldn't be surprised if someone did do that to her. As I watch her, I see a few boys throwing pieces of paper at her hair, trying to see if they can make them land on top of her head. When they notice me walking over to her, they stop their cruel little game as I smile warmly at her as I get closer.

"Hi there." She jumps slightly at the sound of my voice and looks as if she is about to run away again, so I stop her by saying something. "Sorry for scaring you. My name is Colomba, we met yesterday in the hallway, remember?" She lowers her head and nods frantically, looking anxiously at the line of cars full of parents waiting to take their kids home. I know that she is looking for her parents' car, hoping that they will come and rescue her from this conversation with me. "What's your name?"

"Jade Elizabeth." She manages to whisper, not even looking at me as she speaks. I see her hands tighten around her books in her discomfort.

"Well I've never met anyone with two first names before. I'm glad to meet both Jade and Elizabeth." She smiles softly at my little joke even though I thought it was a little weak. A car horn blares behind me, I turn around to see the man from the photo that Jade Elizabeth had in her book sitting in a car. He waves at Jade Elizabeth, signaling for her to come into the car. He must definitely be her father. "I guess I'll see you later, I hope we can have more time to chat again." Jade Elizabeth tries to smile at me, but it looks more like a grimace, as she glances up at me for a second. The car horn blares again.

"Hey Jeje, it's time to go! We have work to do!" Her father yells out.

"Jeje? That's a really cute nickname." She lowers her head and I can see her blushing furiously.

"Thanks." She whispers under her breath before she turns around and runs to her father's truck, almost leaping into the seat and slamming the door behind her. My heart sinks in my chest as I watch her hide her face from my gaze as her father gets into the car after her and starts driving away toward the zoo.

How can I help a girl who can barely even look at me when I talk to her and runs away when I try to start a simple conversation? This seems impossible, but I can't let that stop me. The Crow said that he wants to end bullying and I know that he will do anything in his power to do so. I want to end it in a better way, the right way. To do this, I need to be patient and willing to go the extra mile to reach my goal. I know that someone like her would be the perfect one for the Crow to want to use for his purpose and I need to make sure that she stops getting bullied before the Crow notices the target on her back. Alex walks over to me with his big grin back on his face.

"I told you she's a freak. There's no use in bothering with her, she'll just keep running away from you." He wraps his arm around my shoulder, "Besides, there are other people who would love to spend time with you, and I promise I won't run away." I look up at him, feeling frustrated at my failure.

"Well I can't promise the same thing." With that said I walk away, heading for my bus. Sitting down in my usual seat, Nat and Luis soon join me. Their smiles disappear when they notice that I look upset.

"Hey what's wrong with you?" Nat asks me as she sits beside me.

"Do you remember that girl that I helped pick up her books the other day?" She looks up, something she does when she is trying to think.

"You mean the one who works at the zoo with the tigers?"

"Yeah, that's the one."

"Well, what about her?" I look away from them both, knowing that I will sound stupid.

"I tried talking with her, but she ran away from me again." I'm not surprised to hear Nat laugh. "It's not funny Nat."

"It kind of is when you think of it, I mean I would run away from you too, you are super scary." I lightly punch her arm while I feel myself beginning to smile, seeing how this must sound to her.

"Shut up you jerk." Luis looks at the two of us, obviously confused since I didn't tell him about Jade Elizabeth, or Jeje.

"What are you two talking about?"

"The other day Colomba helped a girl pick up her books and now she's trying to be friends with her. It's not going well to say the least." I glare playfully at Nat.

"Thanks a lot, you are such a great source of support. What would I do without you?" She grins at me mischievously.

"Wither and die, wither and die." We all laugh at her words, me included, no longer able to control myself.

"Who is this girl you're trying to be friends with?"

"Her name is Jade Elizabeth; she has long brown hair and wears a hooded sweatshirt that she always hides her face with. She's super shy and has a hard time talking to, or even looking at, anybody." I notice Luis' eyes grow a little as I describe her. "Do you know who I'm talking about?" He nods his head at me.

"Yeah, I know of her. I've never talked to her before, she would probably run away from me too if I tried to talk to her." He looks away from me for a moment, as if uncomfortable by what he is about to say. "Why are you so eager to be her friend?" I find myself looking away from him too, also feeling uncomfortable.

"Well, I think she just needs someone to help her. She always looks as if she is afraid of the world. I don't want her to be afraid anymore, I want to see her happy." He smiles at my words.

"That's really sweet for you to do for her." I smile back at him.

"Thanks."

"I don't think it will work though." My smile instantly disappears.

"What do you mean?"

"Well- uh… well I think that someone like her needs more than just a friend to make them happy. From what I can see she gets picked on a lot. I don't think that having one friend can make that stop." I look him in the eyes, and I know that he is telling the truth. I take a moment to think about how I can respond to that. It takes an entire minute before I can come up with something.

"Maybe having a friend can give her the strength to keep going despite all that and make her enjoy her life more so that she isn't afraid all the time." Even though that's what I say, I doubt my own words. Can I really change her life so much by just being her friend? Can I help her be stronger by giving her my support? And can her bullying end if I stand by her side? I almost sound a bit silly thinking that it is possible. How can one person change someone else's life so drastically? I force that thought out of my mind, if I don't believe in myself and my mission as Silver Dove then I will never defeat the Crow and make my school a better place.

As the school bus leaves the school parking lot, I change the subject. Talking about something weird I had seen in the hallway and a new book that I had started reading. Luis laughs and talks enthusiastically along with Nat and I, seeing that I feel hope again. When I met Luis on the first day of school, he was so shy he could barely talk to anyone. Now he is opening up and smiles whenever I am with him. He may still be shy when he is around other people, but it is at least a start. Knowing that this has been done with Luis by being his friend, I am now sure that I can do the same thing with Jade Elizabeth.

It doesn't seem like very long before the bus pulls up in front of my mailbox. When I stand up to leave, Luis gently takes my hand in his. I look back at him to see him smiling warmly at me.

"Don't worry Colomba, I know that things will work out for that shy girl. Just wait and see." I smile back at him.

"Thanks Luis." He releases my hand and I step away from my two friends so that I can head home. I feel my heart leap with joy as I look at my house; it is a small place, but a beautiful one in my eyes.

Flowers cover practically every inch of the front yard while flowered vines cover one side of the house. The entire place smells like flowers. I can't think of a more beautiful place than my home. I walk on the stone path that cuts through the giant mass of flowers to reach my front door. When I walk through the front door, I immediately feel relaxed.

"Tesoro, is that you?" I hear my grandmother's voice coming from the living room.

"Yes, I'm home." She steps into the entry area with a smile on her face when she sees me.

"Fantastic, then you can help me finish up this quilt. I could use some help sewing the border along the edge." I give her a big hug.

"I'd love to help." As we walk into the living room where she has the new quilt that she is making spread out, I sit down beside her, taking up a needle and some thread as I begin to help sew on the border.

"How was school today?" I smile warmly as I think about what Luis told me before I left the bus.

"Today was great. I think that you were right, I think I can make a difference at my school as Silver Dove." She grins at me playfully as she sews the corner of the quilt.

"Of course, I was right. I'm your grandmother, I'm always right." I laugh as I complete a few stitches.

"Very funny Grandma." She nudges me playfully with her shoulder and I do the same back to her. As we finish the quilt together, I smile believing that there is hope again.

Chapter Ten

Luis-
Nat Suspects

I watch Colomba as she walks up her driveway toward her house which I can't see since it is hidden behind a group of trees. I meant what I said to Colomba. Things will work out for that shy girl, but it won't be because of one person's kindness. No matter how kind Colomba is, it will be because I will give her the strength to fight against her bullies. I want to believe that Colomba can make things better for that girl, but from my experience it will take a lot more than one person becoming this girl's friend to make things better for her. I want to make this school a better place, so that people like me can go to school without any fear. Then I won't have anything standing in my way to make Colomba my girlfriend.

As the bus begins to pull away, I still keep my

eyes on Colomba until she is out of my sight. Only then do I look away from her to see Nat staring at me, smiling with an all-knowing look.

"What?" She chuckles at me.

"Really? You think I can't see what's going on here?" I look in her eyes, trying to get some kind of clue as to what she's talking about, but I can't find anything.

"I don't understand what you mean." She groans at my ignorance.

"Oh, come on, I see the way you look at Colomba. Did you think I wouldn't realize that you like her?" My mouth suddenly goes dry and my throat tightens as I feel my cheeks burning in embarrassment.

"I don't know what you mean." My voice comes out weak, and even I can tell that I am being unbelievable. She practically glares at me for lying to her.

"Don't act like I'm stupid Luis; you look at her all the time, you are always trying to be the one standing next to her, and you practically hang on every word she says. It's kind of obvious that you care a lot about her." I turn away from her, not wanting to look at her. I know that I can't hide from her anymore, she sees right through me.

"Does Colomba know?" From the corner of my eye I can see Nat grinning in triumph at having me admit my feelings.

"Of course not, Colomba may be a smart girl, but she's a real idiot when it comes to people and their feelings. I don't think she would understand that you love her if you literally spelled it out for her." I feel both relief and disappointment at her words. I am relieved because Colomba doesn't know, and I don't have to live with that embarrassment, but I am also disappointed because of what Nat said. Is Colomba really so clueless about love that she would barely notice my love for her even though it is completely obvious to her best friend? Does she not care about love at all? Or does she think so low of me that she wouldn't bother to notice that I care about her? When I finally have the courage to look up at Nat again, I find her staring at me with impatience and curiosity.

"Are you going to tell her?" She laughs.

"Please, I told her right after you guys first met that I thought you have a crush on her, but she didn't believe me then and I doubt she would believe me now if I said it again." I breathe a sigh of relief that makes her chuckle.

"What are you going to do now that you know for sure that I like her?" She smiles at me sadly, as if she pities me. I want to jump out of the moving bus seeing her pitying me. I can't stand people pitying me, it makes me feel pathetic. Since people are always picking on me, I probably should be used to people pitying me by now.

"Nothing, I guess. I just wanted to make sure. What are you going to do?" I shake my head.

"I don't know. I've never really cared about anyone like I do for her. I'm absolutely terrified by the thought of telling her how I feel. I'm not even really worthy of being her friend, let alone her boyfriend. What do you think?" She smiles at me warmly.

"I think that that is one of the sweetest things I have ever heard. Why do you think you don't deserve her though?" I turn away from her, not wanting to look her in the eyes when I say this.

"She's the kindest, most beautiful, most intelligent girl I have ever met, while I am just an ordinary guy. Most people at the school think of me as less than ordinary. She probably deserves someone better than me." I feel my hands clench into fists on the bus seat and my heart seems to clench as well as I think of the reality of what I just said. I really don't deserve her. How could I ever be worthy of her when the world sees me as something so pathetic, so worthy of being picked on and bullied every day? Maybe when I have triumphed over all the bullies as the Crow, maybe then I will be worthy of Colomba. Maybe then, but not now. To my surprise, Nat actually laughs at what I say. My clenched fists tighten on the bus seat, "Why are you laughing at me?" I ask, insulted by her laughter.

"Because you are so wrong; you are a sweet

guy and you act as if you would do anything for Colomba just to see her smile. Most girls would be happy to have a guy like you in their lives. You shouldn't be so hard on yourself." I am stunned into silence by her words; is that what she really thinks? Am I someone that a girl would want to be with? What do I have to offer Colomba besides the fact that I like her? I'm not what girls probably fantasize over. I'm not athletic, I'm not very confident, I'm not very good looking, and I'm not very smart. I'm great when it comes to English and art, but in math and science I am pretty average. Sometimes I have to struggle just to pass the classes. When I look up at Nat I feel as if she is telling me the truth, but I still can't believe her. Thankfully the bus pulls up to my stop, ending our conversation.

"Thanks for that Nat, I'll see you tomorrow." I say all that very quickly as I grab my stuff and dart out of the bus, not wanting to hear her say anything else to me, knowing that it would only make me feel worse. I run into my Uncle Diego's shop where he is currently cleaning some antique glasses. He smiles when he sees me walking through the door.

"Hola Tigre." He says happily, "How were your classes today?" He always asks me this, but I always see fear in his eyes when he asks. He is always afraid that I will come home and tell him about how I had been picked on that day. That's why I don't always tell him about some of the things that the other kids do to me. I don't want to see him upset. I feel bad about having to lie to the man who raised me, but it feels better to lie to him than to disappoint him. Today though, thankfully, I don't have to lie that much. Nothing really happened today with my bullies.

"Today was good, hung out with friends, nothing unusual." I can almost hear him breathe a sigh of relief, knowing that nobody messed with me.

"That's good, I'm glad that you are making friends this year. Just make sure that they are good friends." He stares down at me with a serious expression and I instantly understand what he means. There have been multiple times when I thought I had made a friend and then they just ended up becoming my bullies too. He is just trying to remind me about that, so I can stay on my guard and make sure that the friends I have now won't turn on me too, but I know that Colomba would never do that to me. She is much too kind to ever do anything like that to anybody. I smile at him, trying to be reassuring.

"Don't worry, these are good people. I think they really like me." My uncle's serious expression leaves his face as he smiles at me mischievously.

"Does that include the Colomba girl you are always talking about?" I feel my hands tighten into fists at my side.

"Shut up about her. She's just a friend, and I haven't been 'always' talking about her." Ever since I first mentioned Colomba, Uncle Diego has been constantly bugging and teasing me about her. Honestly, he's driving me nuts with this, and having him do this only moments after my conversation with Nat isn't really helping my sanity.

"Alright, whatever you say." He says sarcastically, a smile still on his face while I head upstairs to our apartment. I go into my room, but I don't put my hand on the medal to release Shadow like I usually do. Right now, I want silence and privacy.

Going over to my desk, I open one of the drawers and pull out an old photograph. In the picture, my Uncle Diego is at the top of a mountain hiking trail standing beside two other people, my mother and father. The photo was taken only a year before I was born, my uncle told me that they were going to set up a picnic at the top of the mountain to celebrate my mother's birthday. Sitting down at my desk, I stare at the smiling faces of my parents, wondering what they would think of me if they were alive today. Would they be sad that I am always getting picked on by the other kids at school? Would we be happy together as a family? And would they be proud of what I am planning on doing with my powers to help other kids like me? Would they approve of my plan? Or would they hate everything I am doing, just like my uncle, who complains about me whenever the news station talks about the Crow?

I have always tried to do things that I know would make my parents proud, as well as my uncle, who has acted like my parent ever since my parents died in that car crash when I was a little kid. I have always tried to get good grades (even though I find it really hard to do that), I always do what my uncle says, and I try to be a good person. Maybe it is because I always try to be a good person that it is hard for me now to start my plan. I know that I will scare people with what I plan to do with that Jade Elizabeth girl, but I know that it will be for the greater good. People will have better lives because of it. In the end nobody will get bullied anymore. Doesn't that make up for the fear I will give people?

Things might start off bad, but it will end better than before. I think that makes it all worth it. I can only hope that my parents would feel the same way. Maybe I have to be the bad guy for a while so that good things will happen. Maybe once things are better for everyone, maybe then people will see me as the good guy. Maybe they never will. I sigh, closing my eyes so that I can't look at the picture as I think about this. What if I am always seen as the bad guy? What if I am doing the wrong thing? Could I ever make up for what I am going to do?

My mind flashes back to a memory from

Kindergarten. Until a short time before Alex had been my friend, but everyone had singled me out as the weird kid in class, so Alex started joining them in making fun of me. We were on a field trip to a nature reserve and we were all sitting on the grass in a field, having lunch. I had opened up my lunchbox to find a sandwich, a box of juice, and an apple; I remember smiling because that was the only bright side of my day. Most kids look forward to field trips, but I just wanted the day to end because the class spent most of the little hike we did that day throwing twigs at me and tripping me on the trail. One kid even pushed me into a thorn bush while the teacher wasn't looking. Eating my lunch in peace was the only thing that day that felt positive. That, of course, did not last long.

I felt someone slap the back of my head. I closed my eyes in pain and while I was momentarily distracted, someone snatched the sandwich right out of my hand. Opening my eyes, I looked behind myself to see one of Alex's friends throwing my sandwich into the woods while Alex himself grabbed my juice box and apple and took a bite out of it right in front of me. While he was chewing, he glanced down into my now empty lunchbox and smiled.

"You not hungry today or something Louie?" He asked me mockingly. He walked away without waiting for my answer, laughing maliciously while his friends followed after him, joining in with his laughter. If Alex had stayed to hear my answer, he would have found out that I was actually hungry. I spent the rest of the day on that field trip with a growling stomach. It was on that day that I realized that things weren't going to get better for me for a long time. Alex had only stopped being my friend for around two weeks by that point and he was already treating me so terribly. After that day I knew that he was never going to be my friend again, like I had been hoping. I also knew that I may never get another friend because they would abandon me just like Alex did.

I open my eyes and place the picture back into the drawer without looking at it before I slam the drawer closed. No, I will not let that happen to anyone again. I won't let anyone have to deal with the pain I had to live with. I no longer care if I am going to be seen as the bad guy. If I can make other peoples' lives better than mine, then it will be worth it. I just need to wait and find the right moment. I just need to wait until that girl, Jade Elizabeth, is at a point where she will be willing to help me with my goal. To make her willing, I just need to wait until someone at school hurts her again. From what I have seen, I don't think that will take very long.

Chapter Eleven

Colomba-
The Poster

Walking into gym class, I am immediately met by Alex who greets me with his usual smile.

"Hey there, how's it going?" I smile at him as well.

"I'm okay, how are you?" This simple question brings out a long answer that I try to pay attention to, but have a problem doing so. I'm busy thinking about that girl, Jade Elizabeth, Jeje. I have been trying to find her all day, but I have had no luck. I guess when you spend all of your time avoiding people like she does, you learn how to hide pretty well. After what Luis said on the bus yesterday I am starting to feel better about trying to befriend Jeje. I feel as if Luis gave me some confidence with his words.

As we walk over to where the rest of our class

is, we notice that they are all staring at something on the wall. Everyone talking over each other in fear and excitement. Alex stops talking to look down at me with curiosity and I look back at him with the same confusion. We both run over to the crowd and the crowd seems to part to let Alex and I make it to the front of the crowd where we both stare in absolute shock at what we see. On this wall is a painted mural of our school with the school mascot, the Drew's Hollow Horseman, sitting on top of his horse in front of the school. The painting of the school has always been there, a simple show of school pride. Something is different though, hanging right above it is a banner with a large image that I know the school wouldn't have allowed to be hung up anywhere near school property.

Hanging above the painted school is a massive crow, its wings are spread out wide in flight, flying above the school with its talons reaching down, as if it is going to grab the school in its claws and rip it apart. The beak of the crow is open wide, as if it is letting out a silent call, or preparing to attack something, or someone. The crow seems to glare down at anyone who looks at it with menace, as if it is daring you to challenge it. My heart seems to quicken its pace as I look at the crow, but it races even faster when I see something above the crow. Written above the image, in bright red letters, is the message Beware the Crow's Return. I look to Alex, hoping that he has some kind of explanation for what I am seeing.

"Is this some kind of joke?" My voice comes out weak and frightened. Alex notices this and smiles down at me, trying to comfort me.

"Don't worry, Beautiful, you don't have to worry about the Crow trying to hurt you. I'll protect you." He tries to wrap his arm around me, but I back away from him as the coach, Mr. Matthews, walks over to the crowd. Probably curious about what we're all looking at. When the coach sees the image, his entire face turns red in either fury or frustration, I can't tell which.

"Whoever put this up needs to speak up now or else when I find out who did this, I will make their punishment ten times worse." His voice is soft and full of anger and everyone in the class notices this since they all share my terrified expression. He looks from one person in the class to the next, but nobody speaks up. *"Who did this?!"* He screams in rage, but still nobody speaks up, I can see his hands, clenched into shaking fists at his sides. "Alright, everyone is to sit on the bleachers for the entire period, nobody is allowed to speak or do anything, just sit there and whoever did this, I want you to think about how stupid this was." He points to the banner over the painting of the school while the entire class goes and sits on the bleachers. I follow behind the crowd while I hear the teacher on his phone, talking to someone in the front office of the school. He's telling them about what happened and asking them to check the school security cameras to see if they can see who did it. I look back in surprise when I hear him yell out, *"What do you mean the cameras in the gym are busted?! Why wasn't I told about this?!"*

I walk away quickly and sit down on the bleachers with the rest of the class while the angry conversation continues behind me. Alex sits down beside me, and it only takes him a moment to start inching his hand closer to mine. I know that he is going to try and hold my hand, so I move my hands onto my lap and try to ignore him so that I can think about this.

Nat told me that there were some people who supported what the Crow did, and promised to do, but I didn't think that they would do something like that. Why would someone even want to do that? I wrack my brain trying to figure out an answer, but nothing comes. Why would someone risk getting in trouble just so that they could put up a banner like that? The coach ends his call and walks over to us. From his angry expression I can already see that things did not go his way and I doubt that he will be able to catch who put up the banner. He glares at the entire class for a few seconds before he addresses us.

"Today everyone is to stare at that poster," he

points angrily at the poster of the crow over the school. "I want everyone to look at it to remind them about how stupid it was for that person to put it up. Because of that person, everyone in this class will be sitting on the bleachers for the rest of this week with no talking, no cell phones, and no complaining." Despite his no complaining rule, several people make their complaints known, but the coach makes them be quiet and the entire gym is trapped in silence while the coach stares at the poster in rage.

The coach keeps his promise, keeping a close eye on everyone to make sure that we don't do or say anything. This is good for me since I want some time to think to try and figure out who put up the poster. I was one of the last people to enter the gym, so I didn't see any kind of evidence before everyone else had already gathered around the poster. As I think about this, I realize that it would have taken some time to put that poster up. The person would have had to grab a ladder, put up the poster, and then put the ladder away without anyone catching them. There isn't enough time between classes for anyone to have done that right before class. My class is the first gym class of the day, so there are two class periods before where the person could have done this, giving them plenty of time. As I think about this, trying to narrow down the list of suspects. I realize that anyone could have done this and judging from the fact that the security cameras in here aren't working like the teacher said, they may never find out who did it. I already feel a headache forming in my frustration. How, as Silver Dove, am I going to be able to stop the Crow and stop people from supporting him if I can't even figure out a simple prank like this? I feel like a failure as a superhero already and I've had the pin less than a month. How pathetic can you get?

Alex ignores the coach's warning. He leans over and starts to whisper in my ear.

"Are you scared of what was on that poster?" I look over to the coach. He seems to have noticed that Alex is whispering to me, but he looks the other way, pretending not to notice. Apparently, being the star player of two of the school's sports teams has some advantages. One of them being that the coach will ignore it if you break a rule or two.

"A little." I whisper back to him, being completely honest. I am scared of that poster because I know what it means. The Crow has loyal followers in this school, ones willing to get in trouble just to put up a poster to show their support. What else would his followers be willing to do to help the Crow fulfill his mission? Alex leans in closer to me.

"I meant what I said earlier. You don't have to worry, I'll protect you." I look up at him to see that he is smiling his usual charming smile at me. I try to smile back at him, but even I can tell that it probably looks halfhearted.

"Thanks Alex, but I can take care of myself." He tries to hide a smirk and I can feel my hands clenching into fists. He doesn't think that I can defend myself! He thinks that I'm weak and need to be protected! What does he think I am, some kind of damsel in distress!?

I have told Alex before about how I have been doing martial arts for years, it infuriates me to know that he thinks I'm not strong enough to be able to defend myself. Sadly, this happens a lot. People think that I can't take care of myself because I am small. Even though they know that I have been taking martial arts for years, they think I always need help, like I can't do things on my own. It's one of the few things that makes me really mad.

"Of course you can." Even though he says that I can, his tone tells me that he doesn't think I can. "But if you do need any help when that creep Crow shows up again, I will be here for you." He tries to lean in closer again, but I move away, not wanting to be near him.

Thankfully the bell rings, ending the class and saving me from smacking Alex across the face. I quickly pick up my things and hurry out of the gym before Alex can even pick up his backpack. It is a bit mean to avoid him like that since I know he likes chatting with me while walking to our next classes, but I don't really want to talk to anyone right now. First, I am already angry with him and if he keeps talking then I really might smack him. And second, I want to have a few moments to myself to think about this more. What am I going to do about that poster?

Glancing around the hallway, I try to look at each person I pass, and I wonder if they are a supporter of Silver Dove or the Crow. I can't tell just by looking at them and I know this, but I am afraid. I feel as if I am drowning in the crowd. How can I protect all of these people if some of them support the person who I am protecting them from? What am I supposed to do if the people who support the Crow start rising up against me and fight me? I can't hurt them. They are just being fooled by the Crow. So how can I win if I can't even fight them to defend myself? I feel my hands tighten around my books and I know that I will need to calm myself down before I turn myself into a nervous wreck. The problem is I can't figure out a way to calm myself. My mind is just too wrapped around this problem to be able to forget it. What am I going to do?

It doesn't take me long to get to my next class, but the questions still don't leave my head. The teacher starts the class and I try to take notes on what they're saying, but it is hard to do that while my mind is filled with questions that I can't answer.

My headache only gets worse as the class goes on until it feels like someone is beating a hammer against my brain. I close my eyes as the pain gets worse. I wish that this day could just end, and it isn't even lunch yet. I release a soft moan as I open my eyes and try to ignore the pain as the teacher goes on with the lesson and I try my best to pay attention. I take notes as if nothing is wrong even though I know that the gossip about that poster will soon be spread all throughout the school.

Chapter Twelve

Luis-
Jade Elizabeth

When I am through making the finishing touches on my drawing of a crow for art class, I pull out my cell phone to do a little research. Not research for a class, but research for my extra-curricular activity as the Crow. I go onto A-Streamer, a social media website that is popular at my school, and I look up that girl I had seen getting picked on the other day, Jade Elizabeth. It is surprisingly not that hard to find her. Apparently, there are not many people with her name in the area. That part I don't find very surprising though. I've never even heard of that name before. Where do parents come up with names like that? Did they just not want to name their daughter an average name, so they decided to combine two names instead? I don't know the answer, but that's the best I can come up with.

When I open up her profile, I already notice something a bit out of the ordinary. According to her profile, she hasn't been on it for almost a year and her profile barely has anything on it. It's almost as if she just made this profile because someone wanted her to, so she just put the bare minimum down on it with just a few pictures and a very brief bio about herself.

Even though her profile barely has anything on it, and she hasn't even been on it in a while, it hasn't stopped a ton of people from writing cruel things there. All over her page are insults that range from calling her a freak to things I wouldn't even want to say out loud. How can people be so mean to a girl who has probably never even said a word to them? With this girl's extreme shyness, I wouldn't be surprised if she really has never talked to any of these people. They talk about her as if they know everything about her and only see terrible things. Her profile reminds me of the old one I had. Now I use one with a fake name on it so that nobody will know that it's me. I'm safer that way.

I know, it's just a feeling I have in my gut, that this is the girl who will become my first soldier. As the Crow, I can give people superpowers. I can give her the power to fight back against all of these people that pick on her and fill her social media page with hurtful words. The only problem is trying to figure out when the right time would be to give her these powers and what kind of powers I should give to her. I think that the kind of powers I should give to these people should reflect who they are, because this is their battle. I want them to fight as themselves and not just some super-powered person I just made up, that just wouldn't seem right.

As the Crow, I can only give the powers to people if they are willing to accept it, so I need to find a time when this Jade Elizabeth girl will be the most upset by her bullies and will then accept her powers willingly. To do that I will need to wait until right after she has been picked on by somebody, then she will be ready. Right after getting picked on, she will be angry and upset enough to want to fight back. I can't give her the powers when she is calm or else she might not accept the powers. As I glance through her tiny profile, I try to figure out what would be a good superpower for her. Her bio only has simple things like her favorite color and food, while her pictures are mostly of her and her dad. As I scroll through her pictures, I start seeing something similar about each one. All of them seem to have been taken while she was at her job in the zoo. In each picture, she is with at least one of the tigers. So that must be what her job is at the zoo, taking care of the tigers. I smile when I look at one particular photo, one of the few photos where she is showing a true smile. In the photo she is holding a tiger cub who is only as big as a regular house cat.

When I finally notice this similarity in her pictures, the pieces finally fall into place in my head. I smile fully as I suddenly realize what she should become with her superpowers. I notice Alex getting up from his chair to start moving toward the pencil sharpener at the front of the classroom, so I quickly place my drawing of a crow into a folder so that he won't see it and try to do something to it. It wouldn't surprise me if he would try and spill something on my drawing just because my drawing is good while his is absolutely awful.

Even though I am still hiding from Alex, I smile, knowing that this might end soon. Once people start to realize that they can't bully any of these kids anymore, then maybe we can all get some peace and we won't have to hide anything anymore. Maybe people will finally start accepting each other for who they really are. As the Crow I can finally bring peace to our school.

Chapter Thirteen

Colomba-
The Drawing

The bell rings and I practically sprint out of the room, my mind still running through everything that had happened in gym class earlier. Just as I had thought, everyone is talking about that banner as I walk through the hallway. Some people talk about it with fear in their voices, scared about what will happen when the Crow does return like he had promised. What I am really worried about is the fact that some people seem to be happy about that banner. From what I have overheard from people who support the Crow they can't wait until he comes back. I have heard them say that when he comes back the bullies and mean kids in our school will finally get what they deserve. How can anybody be so mean to say something like that?

Nobody deserves to have anything bad done to them, whether they are a nice person or not. This entire situation is so frustrating that I feel like pulling my hair out, but I would rather not be bald at fourteen, so I choose to leave my poor hair out of this. As I think about that, a friendly voice calls out behind me.

"Hey Colomba." I look behind myself to see Luis coming up to me, a big smile on his usually timid face.

"Hey Luis, what's up?" He smiles down at me, his eyes lit up in happiness behind the curtain of his hair.

"Nothing much, just got out of art class." I try smiling back at him despite all of the troubling thoughts swirling in my mind like a tornado.

"You must really love that class. You look happier than a kid who just walked into Disneyland." He chuckles.

"Yeah I do. I finished a project in there. Would you like to see it?" My smile is real now as I respond to him.

"Yeah, I would love to see it." Luis is a wonderful artist, I always love seeing his projects. No matter what he makes, it is always beautiful. I wouldn't be surprised if he grew up to become a great artist that people would pay to see his paintings and drawings hung up in a gallery. He pulls out a large sheet of paper from a folder and holds it out in front of me to see, I hold back a gasp of shock at the drawing.

Spread all over the page is a massive crow, it has its wings spread out wide in flight as it opens its beak to let out a cry. Its talons are spread out in front of it, as if it is about to battle against something. You can see practically every feather of the crow in detail. It almost looks realistic, as if it is about to fly off the page. In the crow's eyes it appears calm, as if it isn't even concerned that it is about to fight someone. It is a very well-done drawing, and it shows his amazing skill, but I can't bring myself to compliment him on it. I stare at it, suddenly feeling sick to my stomach.

When I look at his incredible drawing, I find myself thinking about the poster that had been put up in the gym. The poster in the gym made the crow look far more intimidating while Luis' crow looks more majestic and kind of cool, but they still look pretty similar. As if they were made by the same artist. Is Luis the one who put the poster up? I've heard Luis talk about how much he supports the Crow. Would he do something like put up that poster? When I look up from the drawing into my friend's proud face, my heart breaks, knowing that he may be one of the people who hates me as Silver Dove. In my pain I do something stupid, I lash out at him.

"How could you draw something like that

Luis?" His proud smile immediately fades from his no longer happy face.

"What do you mean? We were assigned to draw a bird and I chose to draw a crow. There's nothing wrong with it." I shake my head at him, my pain turning into rage.

"Nothing wrong with it? After everything that happened between the Crow and Silver Dove, you don't think that there is anything wrong with drawing his symbol?" Luis' eyes suddenly grow darker, my anger spreading to him.

"Of course, there's nothing wrong with it. The Crow is the one who will actually change this school. He's the one who will make this school better for everyone, including you." I have never seen Luis this angry before. He's usually smiling whenever I see him. There is so much anger in his eyes that I almost feel like backing away. I am scared of my own friend. "Maybe once he comes back and he starts making some changes, then you will change your mind about him." I shake my head at him, wanting to scream at him for being so stupid as to support someone like the Crow and thinking that I may support him too.

"Well I hope that the Crow never comes back. All he will do is cause destruction and still say that he is doing the right thing. I wish all these people will stop begging for him to come back. He just needs to stay in whatever little hole he's hiding in and leave everyone alone." Luis actually glares at me as he shoves his drawing back into his folder, his hands shaking in fury as he does this. This time I do back away a little bit at the sight of his anger.

"Alright then. I'll see you later Colomba." He says this in a stiff voice, a voice that sounds as if he is holding back many harsh words. He starts marching away from me, his body stiff in rage. After he gets a few feet away from me, he turns back to face me. "You'll see Colomba, the Crow isn't the bad guy. He will make this school better for you no matter what you think of him." With that said, he continues marching off to his next class, leaving me alone in the hallway, guilt suddenly clouding over me as I instantly regret everything I said.

I shouldn't have said that to Luis. I was angry, and I just let it out on him. Luis may have been the one who put up that poster, but I shouldn't have been so mean to him if he did. He is my friend, and I should forgive him if he did do it. Now I have to ask him for forgiveness instead, my second time this week. I just want to run and hide right now. I want to try and escape from my feelings of shame, but I know I can't. I have to get to class and ask Luis to forgive me for my mean outburst as soon as I see him again. My only problem is will he accept my apology?

Ever since the Crow showed his ugly face at

this school, Luis and I have disagreed on whether or not people should support him and his cause. Even though we disagree on this, I want to still be his friend. I like him a lot, he's a very nice guy and he is fun to hang out with and talk to. I would never want to lose him as a friend. If we keep talking about the Crow and Silver Dove though. I'm pretty sure we may never be friends again. We will probably just end up fighting. Maybe we should just try to agree that we shouldn't talk about the Crow and Silver Dove. That might make things easier between the two of us.

As I start walking to my next class again, my mind wanders to a very depressing thought. What if Luis finds out that I am Silver Dove? Would he stop being my friend if he did find out? I almost want to cry at that thought since I know that he may do that. Is he even worth being my friend if he doesn't support what I am doing as Silver Dove? How can I be friends with someone who doesn't support a part of me? I shake my head, knowing why I am friends with him despite this. I like him, and he likes me, we may disagree on this, but it doesn't mean that we have to stop being friends. Maybe he will change his mind about Silver Dove. Maybe then I won't have to be afraid of him finding out. I've always had the feeling that Luis has been bullied a lot in his life. I'm guessing that's why he supports the Crow so much. If I do prove the Crow wrong, will he ever forgive me as Silver Dove? Luis says that Silver Dove just wants to keep everything the same while the Crow wants to make things better for everyone. Can't he see that I am trying to do the same thing as Silver Dove just in a better way than the Crow is doing it? The Crow wants to make things better by scaring the bullies into being better people, but that only makes him an even bigger bully than them.

My grandmother said it very well when I came home that day after our first battle. She said that he is trying to do the right thing in the wrong way. He wants to end the bullying, but he wants to do that through fear. I want to make this school better too, but I will never do it through fear. I want to show everyone that they can be better people, that they don't have to hurt each other. We can accept each other.

I make it to class and sit down at my chair, resting my head on top of my desk. I just want this day to end already. The teacher comes in to start class and I take my notes as usual, trying to focus on the class while my mind still insists on making me think about Luis, the Crow, Silver Dove, and how the three of them shouldn't mix.

Chapter Fourteen

Luis-
My First Soldier

I march down the hallway, my hands clenched into fists at my side, my anger making every muscle in my body tense. How could Colomba say that about me? I know she said that about the Crow, and she doesn't know that I am the Crow, but it still felt like she was stabbing me in the heart with her words. She said a hurtful comment on the bus the other day about the Crow and I was willing to forget about it because I didn't want to be angry with her, but after what she said just now I know that I have to do something. She believes what most people in this school believe, that I am the evil one. Colomba is a smart girl. I know that if her opinion wasn't being influenced by everything she has heard about me on the news and by other people then she would know that I am really the good guy here.

As I go down the hall, I realize what I have to do. I need to speed up my plan. I can't let Colomba be influenced by everyone else anymore. She needs to see what I will do to help these bullied kids like me. I also can't let down the other kids who are waiting for me to arrive. They have been waiting far too long for me to get a move on and I don't want to keep disappointing them by not showing up. I don't want to disappoint what few fans I have. I am doing this for them and Colomba. Now I will show her what the Crow really stands for. I will show her that I am someone that should be seen as a hero. I am doing something that everyone else is afraid to do, including Silver Dove. Silver Dove is only concerned with keeping things the same as they are now, including all of the bullies. Once I make this school a better place, Colomba will understand and she will love me for what I have done. Running into the bathroom, I quickly make sure that nobody is there, lock the door, and then I place my hand over the Crow Medal and Shadow appears on the bathroom counter.

"Hello Master. How can I help you?" I smile at her, proud of what I am about to say.

"Shadow, it is time to finally help the first to receive our power." Shadow does not appear happy about this. She merely nods her head and says with a defeated sigh, "Tell me what you want me to do." I smile at her even though there is still anger in my heart.

"Transform me into the Crow, Jade Elizabeth is going to finally get what she deserves." Shadow nods again as she begins to fly around me, speeding up quickly until she is almost a black blur. I can almost feel the power growing inside me as I am surrounded by the black blur. I close my eyes for a moment and when I open them, Shadow is gone. Glancing down at myself I see that I have become the Crow again. I laugh in joy, enjoying the feeling of power that I have whenever I have transformed into the Crow. Closing my eyes again, I whisper softly, "Shadow, find Jade Elizabeth." In my mind, I see what Shadow sees. I see her flying through the hallways, but nobody can see her. She is only a shadow.

Shadow keeps flying until she finds the person that she is looking for, a small girl with a large hoodie walking through the halls with her head down. She is probably hoping that nobody will notice her, but I have noticed her. Shadow follows her until she enters the girl's bathroom. Only when she walks in is she alone, that is when Shadow strikes. Shadow flies at top speed, straight into Jade Elizabeth's chest, straight into her pain filled heart. When Shadow is inside her heart, I finally make myself known to my first soldier.

Hello Jade Elizabeth. She gasps and looks

around in terror, but she doesn't see anyone. *Do not worry, I am the Crow and I am here to help you.* She looks around herself and backs into the wall. Since Shadow is inside her, I can hear her thoughts. She thinks that if she can back against the wall then I can't sneak up behind her and attack.

"How can you help me?" Her voice is soft, frightened, as if she thinks I am going to harm her when all I want to do is help her.

I can give you the power to fight back against those who hurt you every day. I know how you feel.

In her mind she is angrily wondering how I could ever understand how she feels. I have power while she doesn't, she gets picked on every day while nobody would dare to mess with someone as powerful as the Crow. She would be surprised if she knew the truth about who I really am behind this mask.

You are afraid to come to school because you know that people will hurt you. You want to have friends, but nobody wants to be friends with the girl that everyone picks on. You want to be strong and confident, like the tigers you and your father take care of in the zoo. I can give you that, all you have to do is let me give you the power and I will let you take your revenge on all those people who hurt you.

Many thoughts race through her mind. She is wondering whether or not I am telling the truth and, if I am, should she do it? Is it the right thing to do? The last question leaves her mind though when she thinks of all the things the other kids in school have done to her, now whether it's right or not doesn't matter to her. All she wants is to make those mean kids feel as scared as she is everyday whenever she has to go to school with them. A smile forms on her lips and her hands curl into fists at her sides.

"I accept, I am ready to be strong." Smiling to myself, I let Shadow take over her. She invades her heart first, feeding off of her anger, feeding off of the darkness that every bully has put into her heart. While Shadow begins to invade her mind, I think of the perfect power to give to her so that she can take her revenge. I chuckle to myself as I hear the excitement in her mind raging, eager to do whatever I say. Laughing in triumph, I give her the power to fight back.

Chapter Fifteen

Colomba-
The Tiger Girl

As class begins, I turn to look at the empty desk beside me, feeling a little sick because of my guilt. Luis usually sits beside me, but he is nowhere in sight. He must have been more upset by what I had said to him than I had thought. I try to bury my face in my book so that I can focus on what I'm supposed to be reading, but I can't pay attention. My mind is too busy thinking about Luis, my heart is breaking as I think of him.

What can I possibly say to him to make this all better? I don't want to lose a good friend because of some stupid fight. The only reason I got so mad at him was because of that stupid poster in the gym. Why was that thing even put up? Why is anyone even supporting the Crow after what he did? I sigh into my book, knowing that I will never be able to figure that out. Some things just don't make any sense.

As I try again to read my book, I hear something from outside the classroom, somewhere down the hall. Lifting my head, I look to the door as I hear the sound coming closer and closer. It sounds as if someone is scraping something sharp against metal. The sound makes my skin crawl, I try to cover my ears, but that doesn't stop me from hearing it. What is that noise? I know that I'm not the only one who can hear this because a lot of the other students in the class are looking up too, confused by what that sound is.

While a few of the other students stand up to walk out into the hallway to find out what the sound is, I stay behind. A familiar feeling has just come over me, the feeling that something terrible is about to happen. Oh no, is this what I have been afraid of starting? Has the Crow finally come back to keep his promise? I stand up from my chair to try and get everyone back into the room, but it is too late. A figure bursts into the room, ramming into people so that they practically fly out of its way, falling to the ground in crumpled heaps. I look away from them to stare at the figure that has now stopped in the center of the classroom, only a few feet away from me.

A girl stands in front of me, wearing an orange hoodie with black stripes all over it, like a tiger. The hood is up on her jacket so that I can only partially see her face, but the part of the face that I can see terrifies me. Beneath the hood appears to be some kind of human-tiger mutant thing. It is shaped like a human face, but orange and black fur covers it. Whiskers coming out of their cheeks like a cat. A tail comes out from under her hoodie that twitches from side to side, as if she is excited by the fear she has caused. Poking out from beneath the sleeves of her hoodie are two hands covered in the same orange and black fur, but what really grabs my attention is that there are sharp claws sticking out of her fingertips.

The girl stares at everyone with a cold, evaluating glare while everyone in the class is frozen in fear. The silence has returned to the room as we all try to figure out who this strange person is in front of us. A chuckle escapes from the tiger-girl's lips as she smirks at all of us, enjoying the confusion she has created. She opens her mouth, throwing her head back to release a terrible roar that sounds like a lion. The room seems to shake from the force of her roar. I cover my ears, but that doesn't help at all. My class runs out of the room, screaming in terror while my fear keeps my feet glued to the ground.

The strange girl snarls at me, letting me see

massive, sharp teeth that make me jump back a little in terror. The mysterious girl pauses for a moment as she stares at me and I look around for somewhere to run away to since I can't transform here without giving away my identity, but I am cornered. There is no way that I can escape from this creepy tiger person. The tiger person moves slightly toward me, their head cocked to the side as if they are examining me. Just when I think that they are about to leap at me and attack, they run away instead. They leave me behind, alone and confused.

The tiger-girl runs out of the room and I follow them to the doorway and watch as they run down the hall, scraping their claws along the lockers and growling at anyone near them. All down the hall, people are screaming and running, trying to get away from the tiger-girl. Even though they are making so much noise, over all of that, I can hear the sound of the claws tearing over the lockers and the growling of a predator echoing through the halls. I try to gather some courage, but the sound of that growling makes me want to run away and hide too, just like the rest of my classmates, but I know I can't do that. I have work to do.

Stepping back into the classroom, I pull out my phone and call the only person that I know who can give me some advice for this. She answers after only a few rings.

"If you are calling me from school without a

good reason you have some explaining to do, young lady?" My grandma says over the phone in a gently teasing tone.

"Grandma, it's finally happened. The Crow has come back, and he's given someone else super powers!" A moment of silence hangs between the two of us for a moment before my grandma asks me very bluntly.

"Well what are you going to do about it?" I feel a bit taken aback by her forwardness, but I answer her anyway.

"I'm not really sure of what to do. I know that the person he gave the powers to is probably one of the bullied kids at school. Since he said that he was going to defend all the bullied kids and help them fight their own battles, that seems like the logical choice." Once again, a moment of silence that makes me impatient with the wait.

"And?" I hold back a sigh of frustration that threatens to escape my lips.

"Well, I can't really fight this person since they are just someone in pain that wants to let out their pain on the rest of the world. They are just lost, and I don't want to fight them because of that. I want to do it another way." I can hear my grandma sighing over the phone. Apparently, she didn't feel the same as I did about holding back my sighs.

"I don't think you have much of a choice Tesoro. When they see you, they will want to fight you and you will need to defend yourself. I must warn you though, the only ways that these people can get rid of their powers is to have the Crow take them away, they get too tired, they get knocked out and the powers fade, or they have to willingly give up their powers. Since we both know how determined the Crow is with his mission, I think the other three options are your best bet. Knocking them out will probably be the easiest option." This time I am the one who sighs. How on earth am I going to do either one of those things? How can I fight them long enough to tire them out? How can I knock them out when I bet they won't let me close enough to do that without scraping those claws across my face? And how can I convince someone to give up superpowers? A lot of people dream of having superpowers, so who would want to give something like that up?

"How am I supposed to do that Grandma?" The silence comes back again, and I know that she is trying to come up with an answer that will comfort me. Apparently, she doesn't come up with one, so she just gives me her most honest answer.

"I'm not sure, Tesoro. You are the one wearing the pin now, it's your turn to make the tough decisions. I'll see you when you get home dear. I am making puttanesca tonight. Good luck." With that said, she hangs up the phone and I am alone again. Well that wasn't very helpful. I was hoping for a bit more advice or something. Grandma is usually good when it comes to advice, but I think I understand what she means. I am responsible for the Dove Pin now. I need to figure out how to use it on my own.

Hiding my backpack in a supply closet, I place my hand over my pin and say the magic words, "Peaceful warrior." I close my eyes as the pin begins to glow and I feel the rush of wind blowing against my face and clothes. I take in a deep breath, hoping that it can give me some courage as I open my eyes to find myself in the armor of Silver Dove. I open my wings out wide, enjoying the feeling of stretching those muscles that didn't exist only moments before. I take in another deep breath as I hear the claws scraping down the lockers again. The sound isn't close, and it sounds as if it is getting farther away from me. The smart thing to do would be to let it keep moving away from me and running in the opposite direction, I have the choice to do this, but I know I can't. I need to fight this thing, no matter how scary the thing is. I almost peed myself in terror when it cornered me in the classroom, I can only wonder why it didn't attack me.

Clenching my fists, I forget my fear as I take off into the air. I fly through the hallways, getting closer to the sound of claws scraping against metal. As I fly through the halls, I dodge past people as they run away from the sound I am chasing. They cheer for me and point at me as I fly past. They are all eager for me to end this as soon as possible, and I will try my best not to disappoint them.

Chapter Sixteen

Luis-
Tigerclaw and
Silver Dove

This is going perfectly. It's even better than I thought. Tigerclaw is running through the halls, scraping her claws down the lockers, roaring and growling at everyone who passes by her. I feel proud of her, knowing that she is finally showing some strength. Since Shadow is inside of her, giving her these powers, and Shadow is a part of me, I can hear her thoughts and see through her eyes as she runs through the halls. She is happier than she has been in a long time. She is no longer afraid to walk among the other students. Now *they* fear her.

You like your new powers, don't you Tigerclaw? I whisper softly in her mind. She lets out another roar before she answers me.

Yes, yes, I do, more than anything.

I smile beneath my mask as I hide in the boy's bathroom that I have locked. Since I am seeing through Tigerclaw's eyes I am distracted. I can still see what is going on around me, but I can't focus on both of them at the same time, one of my weaknesses as the Crow. Because of this, I have to make sure that I am in a safe place, so that nobody will mess with me while I am helping Tigerclaw get her revenge.

Just remember what I told you Tigerclaw. I gave you this opportunity so that you can show my power to everyone. You can get your revenge on the people who picked on you, but you will not hurt any innocent people.

I hear her growling faintly in frustration at my words and her hands clench into fists at her side while her tail twitches from side to side.

Of course, I wouldn't do that. I am not a monster. Didn't you see that I didn't hurt that one girl even though I had her cornered in the classroom?

I take in a deep breath, trying to get rid of my annoyance at hearing the anger in her voice. I am actually really glad that she didn't attack the student she is talking about, especially since it was Colomba. It almost felt like I was going to have a heart attack when I saw who she had cornered in that classroom. I was about to tell Tigerclaw not to attack her when she actually stopped herself and ran out of the room to chase someone else. When I saw her do that I let out a huge sigh of relief. It would have broken me apart if I saw her get hurt by Tigerclaw, the person I created. In my mind, I can feel Tigerclaw's fur covered lips pull up into a smile.

That girl is one of the only people who has been nice to me at this school. I would never hurt someone who was kind to me.

I am not surprised that Colomba has been kind to her. She did tell me on the bus the other day that she wanted to try and be friends with her, hoping that it would make her come out of her shell more and be happier. I thought that she was being a bit unrealistic. Having just one person be your friend doesn't make the pain go away. It may make things a bit better, but not completely. To make it end completely you need to do something a bit more drastic, like what I'm doing with Jade Elizabeth now, or should I say, Tigerclaw.

I did see her defend Jade Elizabeth once in the hallway, but Jade Elizabeth ran away from her. I would have thought that she would be angry with Colomba, not grateful. I suppose that Jade Elizabeth did feel as if Colomba was doing the right thing but was too afraid to show it. Defending someone can help them, but they need to learn how to defend themselves too.

Tigerclaw stops running when a sound reaches her ears. The sound of police sirens wailing in the distance but coming closer. I laugh softly.

It appears that we will be having an audience Tigerclaw. Maybe you should go out and greet them, it would be the polite thing to do.

Tigerclaw laughs at my sarcasm as she heads toward the front doors of the school. Stepping outside, she makes it there just in time to see five police cars screeching to a halt in front of the school, sirens blaring. All of the police officers step out of their cars quickly and point guns at Tigerclaw. Even though they have their weapons pointed at her, I can still tell that they are afraid of her. I can see one young officer practically quivering in his fear.

Tigerclaw smirks at them as they tell her that she needs to surrender. Even though they practically beg her to stop, she keeps slowly moving closer to them. When she is only around twenty feet away from the police, they won't take her disobedience anymore and they open fire. I smile to myself as the bullets bounce off of Tigerclaw's skin.

When I was thinking of what powers to give her, I made sure that invincibility would be one of them. Since I don't have invincibility as one of my powers, I know how important it is. When I had my fight with Silver Dove a while back, I was scared that she would be able to get close to me with that sword of hers. Thankfully I had enough of my shadow dogs to fight her for me.

By the time the police realize that the bullets aren't hurting her, it is too late for them. Tigerclaw sprints up to them and grabs the front end of one of the police cars. She lifts it up as if it is weightless while all of the police officers stare at her with open-mouthed shock. Within a second or two, she has lifted the car up as far as she can and then she tosses the car so that it flips on its top. The police continue to stare at her and I know what is going through their minds. They are wondering who this superpowered girl is. They don't have to wait long though because she answers this silent question for them. She leaps onto the car she flipped over and glares down at the people below her.

"I am Tigerclaw! I am a soldier of the Crow! Anyone who stands in my way will pay!" My soldier lets out a terrifying roar that seems to shake the ground with its power. The roar sends the police

leaping into their remaining cars and driving off or running in any direction away from Tigerclaw. Tigerclaw laughs menacingly before she leaps off the top of the police car and runs back inside the school, scraping her claws down the sides of the lockers as she goes down the halls.

What do you want to do now, my soldier?

She chuckles darkly as she sprints down the hallway, using her new animal-like senses to sniff out and find something.

I know someone who really deserves to face me as Tigerclaw. A girl who needs to learn that she's not better than everyone else.

I feel myself smile as well, when I figure out who she is probably thinking about.

If you are talking about the person I am thinking of, then I will enjoy watching you do this.

She laughs out loud and lets out a roar of joy as she continues to run through the maze of hallways, trying to find her prey.

With her animal sense of smell, she finds the scent easily and tracks down her prey as they try to make their escape from the school through the football field. As Tigerclaw catches her prey in her sight, she lets out a roar of triumph before she takes up the chase. When Angela heard the sound of that terrifying roar, she turned around to see that she was being chased. She tries to run faster, but that is in vain. Tigerclaw leaps high into the air and lands right in front of Angela, scaring her so badly that, as she tries to stop herself from running straight into Tigerclaw, she falls backward into the dirt. Her brown eyes look up at Tigerclaw with more fear than I have ever seen anybody show in my life. It is beautiful.

In Tigerclaw's mind, I hear the joyful thoughts racing through her mind. Angela has been so mean to her ever since this school year started. They have a few classes together and Angela uses that time to make Jade Elizabeth's life miserable. It didn't take Angela long to figure out that Jade Elizabeth would be easy prey. Once she figured that out, she has been harassing her almost every day. Spreading rumors about her, making her feel as if she doesn't deserve to be alive. Angela has teased her about everything from her face, her clothes, her hair, even the way her voice sounds when Jade Elizabeth actually finds the strength inside to actually say anything.

Beneath her is the girl who has been making fun of her the most, the one who has been the cruelest, and now she is scared of her. I can understand how she feels; if I had Alex in the same position, I would feel just as happy. I'm actually a bit jealous of her right now.

Her pleasure is ruined though when a powerful force hits her from the side and she is thrown into the air for a couple feet before crashing to the ground. It takes her a moment to be able to move again after such a powerful strike. When Tigerclaw opens her eyes, she is greeted by the sight of a figure standing over her. As the dust settles, we can both see who it was who knocked her down, Silver Dove.

My fists clench together, and my entire body seems to shake as an uncontrollable rage comes over me when I look at her. How dare she interrupt Tigerclaw when she is finally about to get the revenge she deserves?! She has been wanting this for so long. Why does Silver Dove have to come in and ruin it for her?!

If you want to get your revenge Tigerclaw, you're going to have to take out Silver Dove first. Tigerclaw growls in fury.

With pleasure.

Tigerclaw leaps off the ground, straight at Silver Dove, her claws extended, aimed directly at her face. I smile to myself, the battle has begun.

Chapter Seventeen

Colomba-
Fighting Tigerclaw

I stand over my current opponent who is glaring up at me, their fangs flashing in the sunlight. In a flash, they are back on their feet and leaping at me, their claws reaching for my face. Taking a quick step forward, I use my arms to block their attack and they fall to my side. She growls furiously as she begins to circle around me like an animal trying to find a weak spot on its prey. I turn around with her, making sure that she won't get to my back, anyone's weak spot.

When she sees that I won't let her find a vulnerable spot, the tiger-girl releases a roar of rage before leaping at me again. Lifting one arm with extended claws, I block that blow only to have her other hand reach down and grab my leg. Before I can react, she lifts my leg and I fall to the ground.

The tiger-girl doesn't waste a second. She is on top of me as soon as I have hit the ground. From my position on the ground I can finally see the tiger-girl's face more clearly. Looking beneath the hood I see a familiar pair of beautiful green eyes. I hear myself gasp at the sight of them as I recognize the person I am fighting.

"Jade Elizabeth?" She leaps away from me, her eyes examining me carefully as fear makes her breathing strained, and her eyes grow wide.

"How do you know my name?" Oh jeez. How would Silver Dove know her name? ... I can't think of anything. Okay just ignore the question and hope she won't notice.

"What are you doing Jade Elizabeth? Do you really think that hurting Angela will make you feel better?" When I hear myself say her name, I glance down at where Angela had been, only to see that she has already run away. Good, at least I have kept her safe for now. Jade Elizabeth growls at me in fury.

"My name isn't Jade Elizabeth anymore, I am *Tigerclaw!*" Her words are released in a roar that makes my body freeze in terror, but I try to keep a strong composure as I look at her in the eyes.

"No matter what you tell yourself, you will always be Jade Elizabeth." My voice is stern, almost like a parent scolding a child, even though I feel like a little kid facing a monster from a scary movie. She only growls at my words.

"I am not that weak little girl anymore! The Crow has given me the strength that I have always wanted so that those people won't hurt me again!" She points to the school and I know that she thinks of everyone in there as her enemy, including myself.

"The strength he has given you isn't real though. It won't last forever. Once the Crow leaves you, you will be back to your normal self and the strength he gave you will be gone." She looks surprised and hurt, as if she hadn't thought of that before. A moment of silence falls between the two of us and I let the silence stay, giving her a moment to think this through. Hopefully she can see sense. After a minute has passed, I hear her growl beneath her hood.

"*Liar!*" She lunges at me. I try to dodge her strikes that seem to fly in front of her, faster and faster. I block each strike she throws, and I realize that she is going to keep striking until she finally gets me. Swinging one of my wings forward, I hit her so hard that she flies through the air and lands on the ground, gasping for breath in exhaustion. I feel my heart leap in excitement. Fantastic! She is wearing herself out! If she keeps this up, then her powers will disappear, and she will return to her normal self.

Tigerclaw seems to realize this too since she

quickly gets up and runs back inside the school, and I follow eagerly after her. I won't allow her to let this fight go on all day, I have better things to do with my time. I will end this as fast as I can. Leaping off the ground, I open my wings so that I can fly straight through the school's back doors and follow the sound of Tigerclaw's retreating footsteps. As I fly through the hallways, the footsteps suddenly stop, and I am unsure of which direction to go. Letting myself land, I walk quietly down the hall, straining my ears to try and hear something coming from Tigerclaw.

Passing by the entrance to another hallway, I find who I am looking for, but it is too late. Tigerclaw hooks her claws beneath my armor, and she lifts me off of the ground, throwing me as easily as if I was a child's toy. As I fly through the air, I try to catch myself with my wings, but I am not fast enough. I crash straight through a wall and into a classroom, landing on a large pile of instrument cases. I groan softly as I pick myself out of the mess to find myself in the band room. Brushing some of the rubble from the broken wall off of my shoulders and shaking out my wings, I glance over to my side to see the entire school band staring at me with open mouthed shock. Apparently, I had just interrupted band practice. Smiling awkwardly, I give them a simple wave.

"Hey, how's it going?" Nobody answers me,

they simply keep staring at me in shock. "Well… it was nice talking with you all." I walk through the hole in the wall that I just made so that I can continue to fight with Tigerclaw, who is now running down the hallway, tearing her claws down the lockers on the wall as she goes. "Oh come on! Can't that girl wait ten seconds for me to get back up?" Sighing, I open my wings again to fly after her, trying to catch up after her long head start.

Chapter Eighteen

Luis-
The Battle

I am laughing out loud right now. Tigerclaw just smashed Silver Dove through a wall and is now running down the hallway, scaring everyone who gets close with a ferocious growl. This is just what I wanted, everyone running scared from my soldier, while my soldier finally gets the revenge they deserve, and Silver Dove not being able to defeat them.

Are you enjoying yourself Tigerclaw?

I ask in her mind. She responds back almost immediately, excitement in every word.

Definitely. I just hope that Silver Dove stays out of my way. How did she know my name, anyway?

I was actually wondering that myself. How does Silver Dove know who Tigerclaw really is? She must know her somehow. Does she have a class with her? Or does she know her from outside of school? It has always been kind of obvious to me that Silver Dove has to be a student here, but which student is what I want to know. Maybe once Tigerclaw has defeated her, I will finally know. Then I can finally convince her to join my side. We are meant to fight side-by-side since we both share these pins. That's what Shadow once told me, so I might as well let her join the winning side. With her on my side, nobody would be able to stand in our way. All of the mean kids at our school would beg us for mercy, and I might just give it to them, but I also might not. Maybe they don't deserve mercy, maybe they deserve to get pushed around for a bit just like how they've been pushing everyone else around.

I'm not sure Tigerclaw, but once you defeat her we can find out together.

In her mind, I can hear her thinking about what Silver Dove said, about how the strength I have given her won't last forever. Images of her father and the tigers they take care of in the zoo flash through her thoughts. The only time she is confident with herself is when she's with the tigers. When she is with them, she almost feels as if she is with someone who understands her and doesn't judge who she is. The tigers don't care if she doesn't talk that much, they only care about her. She still understands that they are dangerous animals, but since she knows that her tigers have never attacked her, or shown any kind of aggression toward her, then they must care about her in some way. They respect her enough to not attack because she respects and loves them. She feels more comfortable around the tigers than she does other people. I feel enraged, hearing her doubting me in her mind.

What are you thinking Tigerclaw?

I ask her this even though I know the answer. She frantically tries to think of something, not knowing that I have already heard her thoughts.

I was just thinking about what I am going to do after all this is over.

I almost have to laugh, that is what she was thinking. She just made it sound better for me so that I wouldn't get mad at her. Maybe she has realized that since we can talk in her head, I may understand a little bit of her thoughts too. What she doesn't know is that I can hear all of it.

Well, you don't have to worry about that. Once this is over, nobody will mess with you again. You will be safe. You will be free.

She lowers her head for a moment, and I can feel her trying to stop the doubting thoughts from coming into her head. Tigerclaw wants to believe me, but Silver Dove put a bit of doubt in her mind and it refuses to go away.

As I stand in the bathroom, hidden from the rest of the school behind the locked door, I bang my fist against the counter. I'm enraged that my first soldier, the one that I gave the honor of being the first to get superpowers, is already doubting me. Why is she doubting me!? Who does she think she is?! Doesn't she realize that I gave her superpowers? A lot of people would kill to be given superpowers, but she wants to give up after only having these powers for around an hour. Maybe Tigerclaw isn't as smart as I thought. If she is willing to give up having superpowers and the chance to give her bullies the revenge they deserve, then Tigerclaw must be really dumb.

I sigh to myself, trying to let my anger disappear. It doesn't completely go away, but it does weaken a bit. Just because she is doubting me doesn't mean I can't prove her wrong. She will finish her mission, she will see that I am right, and then she will never doubt me again. She will understand that she should never listen to Silver Dove. That is, unless Silver Dove finally gets some sense and joins me in my cause.

One day, Silver Dove will realize that I am right, that I am the one she is meant to follow. I am stronger than her, I think we both know that. It is only right that she should be the one to follow me. It may not be today, it may not be tomorrow, but one day Silver Dove will follow me, and we will make this school a better place.

As Tigerclaw makes her way through the school, I hear people scream in fear at the sight of such a terrifying monster. They fear my creation. She roars and growls at them, starting to enjoy her role as Tigerclaw again. I smile to myself. I don't need to worry anymore about this. Tigerclaw is back to creating some terror for everyone and Silver Dove has apparently given up the fight. I am so close to victory. This is probably the only time in my life that I can actually say that. As Tigerclaw swipes her claws done some posters on the wall, I laugh to myself in the bathroom, laughing at my victory.

Chapter Nineteen

Colomba-
Ending the
Battle

Speeding through the air, I search for Tigerclaw, following the sound of her claws tearing across the floor as she tries to run away from me. In her tired state, it doesn't take me long to catch up to her. I put on an extra burst of speed and I fly right over her head and land in front of her. She forces herself to make a quick stop to not run right into me. She has to drag her claws on the tile floor to slow herself down, making a spine-chilling screeching sound as she does it, creating long scratches down the floor.

"This isn't what you really want Jade Elizabeth, is it?" She growls under her breath while her green, feline eyes flash in anger.

"How would you know what I want? You don't

even know me!" I try to think of some way to respond to that, but she doesn't give me a chance. Her hand lashes out at me, her claws ready to rake down my face. Thanks to years of martial arts training, I now have fast enough reflexes that I block her strike only moments before her claws would hit my face.

"I may not know you, but I can see who you really are! You want to be strong, that's what the Crow must have promised you, to make you stronger! You want to not get picked on anymore because you are shy! He told you that with this power, then you can finally make that stop! Am I right?!" Her green eyes look away from me, afraid of my questions. I know that I'm right. "Don't believe him. You don't need his help to be stronger. *You can do that on your own!*" She lowers her arms and face.

"I was born weak. This is the only way I can be stronger and make all that stop. I need his help." Her voice is so soft and defeated, I almost want to hug her right now, but I know she would probably hit me if I did, so I keep that feeling back.

"Think about the tigers you and your father care for." She glares at me, her intelligent eyes examining me as her hands tighten into fists at her sides.

"How do you know about that?" My body stiffens in fear; how would Silver Dove know that?

Quick think of something!

"I know many things." Well that was a lame excuse. "But think of your tigers, they don't start off strong, they start out as little cubs completely weak to the world! People are the same. You don't start out strong and confident, you have to learn how! If you want to be that way, then that is what you must do. *You must learn!*" Tigerclaw stares at me for a moment, stunned by my words. Her fists loosen until her hands just hang at her side. She lets her head fall so that she is staring at the ground.

"How can I be strong when everybody just enjoys picking on me? You can't feel strong when everyone keeps beating you down." I slowly and cautiously move closer to her, hoping that she is trusting me enough to get close without trying to tear her claws down my face.

"That's when you show your strength by picking yourself back up. If you keep picking yourself back up and stay strong, then one day you will realize that their insults don't hurt as much as they did before. One day you will realize that they don't hurt at all." I am now only a few feet away from Tigerclaw, Jade Elizabeth. Taking a chance, I reach out my hand to hold hers.

To my surprise, she doesn't scratch me with her claws or even move her hand away from mine. Actually, she holds on tightly to my hand, as if she needs the support of my touch. She lifts her head to reveal that tears are beginning to fall through the fur on her face and her whiskers twitch as she holds back sobs.

"It will take a lot of work to get the strength you want, but I'm sure that there are many people out there who will be willing to help you. You just need to push yourself to go find these people. It may be difficult, but it will be worth it in the end, that I can promise." Tigerclaw manages to smile at me through her tears.

"You're right." I smile back at her, "I don't want to do this anymore. I don't really want to hurt anybody. I just want to be myself again." With that said, Tigerclaw closes her eyes and in an instant her fur, fangs, and claws disappear and now the only person who stands in front of me is Jade Elizabeth.

Jade Elizabeth glances down at her hands and sees that there are no longer claws sticking out of her fingertips. When she glances back up at me, she gives me a soft, shy smile and I return the smile as well. Wrapping my arm around her shoulder, I lead her down the hallway and into the principal's office. Inside I can see the microphone on his desk that he uses for announcements. Picking it up and turning it on, I bring it to my lips.

"Don't worry everyone, this is Silver Dove. You can come out of hiding; the threat is gone. The Crow no longer has control over our friend. She is safe as well. Good bye everyone, and good luck because I know the Crow will return. Stay vigilant." With that said, I place my hand over the dove on my armor and say the magic words, "Bring peace little dove."

The dove on my armor flies off my chest and out of the principal's office. I slowly walk after it with Jade Elizabeth at my side. We are now standing in the entryway of the school and the dove flies to the ceiling, which is around twenty feet from the ground. The feathers grow brighter and brighter, I bring my wing in front of Jade Elizabeth and I so that we won't be blinded by the light. Once the light disappears, I lower my wing to see that all of the destruction that was caused by my battle with Tigerclaw is now gone. The school looks as clean as it did this morning.

I smile, feeling proud, as I give Jade Elizabeth a quick hug before I open my wings and fly down the hallway as fast as I can so that I can find an empty room and change back into my normal self before anyone notices that I am missing. As I fly past the rooms, I see students beginning to poke their heads out from where they had been hiding. They all cheer when they see me pass by, I smile wider, knowing that I have done the right thing, that I have saved my school and the people in it from someone who wants to destroy us. I may have been scared out of my mind, but it was worth fighting that battle, knowing that Jade Elizabeth is safe and

happy.

Chapter Twenty

Luis-
My Defeat

No, no, *no!* Why did it have to end that way?! I change back into my normal self while I continue to pace across the floor of the bathroom that is still locked so that nobody can get in. Why did Tigerclaw give in to what Silver Dove said to her? Couldn't she see that Silver Dove was just trying to trick her?

Now that I am back to my normal self, I place my hand over my Crow Medal and Shadow appears, standing on the bathroom counter. She stares at me with a dark look in her eyes, as if she is disappointed in me. I turn my eyes away from her gaze as I continue to pace.

"Sorry to bring you out again Shadow, but I just need someone to talk to." Shadow scoffs at my words.

"You need more than just someone to talk to Master, you need some sense." I clench my fists at my side, but I still don't look at her.

"I thought this would work out with Tigerclaw. Why would she give up so easily?!" Shadow taps her talons against the countertop, making an irritated noise that seems to echo in the empty bathroom.

"She didn't give up, she saw the sense that you are refusing to see. She decided to do the right thing and not lash out at her enemies. *Jade Elizabeth* decided to make herself stronger, instead of just letting you give her power." I noticed how much emphasis she put on Jade Elizabeth's name, obviously trying to point out to me that she is no longer Tigerclaw, no longer my soldier. I glare at her, directing all of my anger at her.

"Jade Elizabeth gave up because she isn't the one I should have chosen to be my first soldier. I should have picked someone who wouldn't have disappointed me. I need someone stronger, someone who won't give up." I make Shadow return to the medal so that I can be alone again.

It was a mistake to bring her out. I should have known she would just try and nag me about what I did. She just doesn't see what I am trying to do. If I can transform these bullied kids, and they get their revenge, then the other kids will be so afraid to pick on each other that the bullying will stop at my school. I am doing the right thing, she is just too blind to see that. Just like Silver Dove.

Shadow told me that Silver Dove and I are meant to work together. That is what we are supposed to do since we both have these magical pins, but there is no way that I will work with her. How can I work with someone who plans on getting in my way every time I try to do something to help everyone? Can't she see that she is the one doing the wrong thing? She's letting all those people who bully kids like Jade Elizabeth and me get away with it. She doesn't want them to get punished.

If someone steals, they go to jail as punishment. Why shouldn't they get punished too for the mean things they have done? Don't people deserve to be punished when they have done something wrong, no matter who they are? Angela has been getting away with her bullying for years since her father is rich and he is now the principal in the school she goes to. Alex has been getting away with it since he is rich as well and also one of the best athletes in the school. Don't they deserve punishment after what they have done to all of the people in this school? Why am I being seen as the bad guy when they are doing these horrible things to people every day and I am the one trying to stop them? It doesn't make sense, yet Silver Dove is trying to protect them anyway. She's an idiot. She's trying to protect the real bad guys here, so why is she the hero to everyone?

Over the intercom, the principal announces that school is over for the day, so we should all head for our buses or call our parents to pick us up. Unlocking the bathroom door, I walk into the hallway, mingling with the other students as they make their way to the buses to head home. None of them aware that they are walking beside the person who caused the destruction and mayhem they had experienced less than an hour ago.

Chapter Twenty- One

Colomba-
After the
Battle

As I walk through the school to head outside to the bus, I pass by the doors to the gym and a sickening feeling buries itself deep in my stomach. After all that happened, I never did figure out who was the one to put up that banner that I saw in gym class. I feel even worse when I realize that it still might have been Luis who put that up. Luis has never hidden his support for the Crow, and he definitely has the artistic talent to have made it. I am afraid for my friend, he is choosing to side with a monster. I don't know how things will end with the Crow, but it frightens me, knowing that one of my own friends supports him instead of me. It's almost as if he wants me to fail as Silver Dove.

A small group of people walks past me, talking excitedly about the battle between the Crow and Silver Dove. From what I hear it doesn't sound as if they had been supporting me. One of them tells his friends that he had hoped that Tigerclaw would have beaten me so that the Crow can get rid of all the mean people in this school. I want to scream at them. I want to tell them that I am just trying to make sure that everybody is safe, that the Crow is doing this the wrong way. I want everybody to be happy and safe too, but *he* is causing mayhem and destruction and trying to make the bullying stop by force. I won't let that happen. I can't! That group moves ahead of me, leaving me alone to brood in silence. Why does it have to be like this? Why do we all have to be divided?

Walking outside the front doors, I find my bus easily and get inside, practically falling down on the seat in exhaustion. My heart is still pounding in my chest from the fear and excitement of the battle. I take in several deep breaths to try and calm myself while other students start piling in the doors. It doesn't take long for a familiar face to come onto the bus, Luis. He gives me a faint smile as he sits down beside me.

As Luis and I sit in silence on the old, beaten bus seat, neither of us mentions what happened earlier with Tigerclaw, the Crow, or Silver Dove and I think I know why. In a way, I think we are both silently agreeing that we shouldn't bring up that subject again. We are good friends, too good of friends to break up over a silly argument about who we support, Silver Dove or the Crow. From now on, I know that I will never bring that subject up with Luis since I know that it will start an argument. Friends can disagree on things, but they shouldn't let that break them apart. If it means that I never talk about Silver Dove and the Crow so that I can keep a new friend, then I will happily do that to make sure that Luis stays by my side.

I start a conversation with him about his uncle's shop and he happily joins it, eager to not talk about what happened at school today. While the bus continues to fill up with students, Luis tells me about his small collection of antiques, but my mind is elsewhere. I look at my friend and I wonder if he was the one who put that poster up. If he was, then how can I be friends with a person who thinks so badly of Silver Dove when I am Silver Dove?! That's like being the president and having a vice-president who voted for somebody else, it doesn't make sense.

Nat comes onto the bus and joins us, helping to relieve some of the tension with some jokes. She somehow senses that we don't want to talk about the battle that just happened, so instead she tells us about the time her cousin got his face smashed into a birthday cake because of a small dog and a very annoyed cat. By the end of the story the three of us are practically rolling on the seats, tears streaming down our faces in laughter. I am grateful to her for giving us this gift of laughter, for giving us a moment to forget about what happened at school today. Sometimes it is nice to try and forget.

It doesn't take too long for the bus to pull up in front of my house. Waving goodbye to my friends, I walk up the driveway to head inside and talk to the only person in the world who can truly understand what I feel right now.

Opening the front door of my house, I am greeted almost instantly by my grandma who pulls me into a warm hug.

"Tesoro, I saw the whole thing on the news, you were wonderful!" I almost feel like laughing at what she says.

"It's on the news already? That's kind of impressive. We only had the battle about an hour ago." She chuckles at my comment.

"Yes, several people caught portions of your battle on their phones, they showed those videos on the news. One person actually showed you talking that Tigerclaw girl down. I am so proud that you were able to stop that girl with very little fighting. I was right, you have made an excellent Silver Dove." I smile in pride at my grandma's words.

"Thanks, I've honestly been having doubts about that myself." She shakes her head at me.

"Never doubt yourself Tesoro, you were made to be Silver Dove, and I have no doubt that you will prove that time and again." I want to be happy about her words, but something that happened before the battle is bugging me and I feel like I need to talk to her about it.

"Grandma, before I fought Tigerclaw, I tried to get some advice from you, but you kind of left me hanging. Why did you do that?" She looks away from me, and I know that she feels a bit guilty for what she did, but she tries to explain herself.

"Tesoro, I am your grandmother, but I can't hold your hand every time you have a problem. I need to let you figure it out for yourself sometimes. It may hurt me to watch you do that, but it will be better for you later on. I may have more experience as Silver Dove, but I need to let you learn how to use your skills to become a different Silver Dove than I was. I had to face very different problems when I had that pin than you will. I can't give you advice for situations I have never gone through, that would be unfair to you." I still want to be angry with her for leaving me to fight Tigerclaw without any advice, but I know that I can't. She is right.

"Okay, I guess I can understand that, but what do I do now? I have fought against the Crow and now I have fought against someone that he has given powers to. I have beaten him twice already, but I can just feel that he won't give up. Am I going to have to keep fighting him forever? When will he stop?" Once again, she shakes her head at me.

"I'm not sure, I don't know him. You just have to keep stopping him until he realizes that he is wrong I suppose." She says this as if it is no big deal while my mind is racing faster than a kid hyped up on sugar.

I am going to be fighting this guy for the rest of my life! The Crow will never give up! How am I supposed to accomplish all of the dreams that I have made for myself (going to college, becoming a doctor, and taking care of my family) when I can't defeat this guy and I have to stop everything I am doing whenever he decides to possess another person and give them powers? What am I going to do? I know I can't ask my grandma this since she doesn't know, nobody knows. It feels like my heart is breaking when I realize that my life is in the hands of the Crow, the hands of a complete lunatic.

Chapter Twenty- Two

Luis-
What Next?

My Uncle Diego and I watch the news now that we have finished dinner. My hands clench the fabric of a pillow sitting beside me in frustration as we watch. They keep showing the same thing on the news, Silver Dove fighting Tigerclaw, my first soldier being defeated. I'm not surprised that the people on the news keep saying rude things about me, referring to me as the monster. While my uncle's eyes are glued to the TV, completely fascinated by the battle, I hear him saying rude things about the Crow under his breath in Spanish. I want to say something in response to him, but I know that he would just start getting upset with me too.

Instead, I choose to leave and go to my room. I tell my uncle good night and make my escape. I don't place my hand over the medal to summon Shadow like I usually do whenever I am in my room. Tonight, I want to be alone.

Even though nobody knows who I really am, I still feel embarrassed by my defeat. Jade Elizabeth was the perfect person for me to choose as my first soldier; she has been picked on for years, she wanted to get her revenge, and I gave her the perfect powers to defeat Silver Dove. The only reason I lost was because Tigerclaw listened to what Silver Dove had to say. Why she did something as stupid as that I'll never know. When she stopped to listen to Silver Dove, I screamed in her head that she needed to start fighting again or everything she had done would have been for nothing and we would lose. Surprise, surprise, I was right.

As soon as she goes back through the doors of our school, Jade Elizabeth is going to be picked on just like she was before, but this time I won't be there to help her. She refused my help the first time, why should I help her again? Since she refused my help, she deserves what she's going to get. If she begs for the Crow's help, I will just laugh. Next time I will choose someone who will actually get something done, someone who will defeat Silver Dove. The only problem is, who will I choose?

Going over to my desk, I pull out my list of bullied kids in the school, trying to figure out which one deserves my help the most. There are so many kids on this list, so many kids who don't deserve to be picked on like they do every day. This is why I am doing this. I am helping these kids. They need someone who will help them fight for themselves.

I set the list back down when I realize that I probably shouldn't make a big decision like that tonight. I am still too upset by my defeat earlier to make a good decision. Instead, I pick up my sketchbook and open it up. On the first page is the picture of the crow that I drew for art class. Colomba had been so upset when I showed it to her, I feel a bit guilty when I think of that. I didn't want to make her mad, but I know that she is a big supporter of Silver Dove. When we were sitting on the bus heading home, we didn't talk about what had happened. I guess we have both realized that if we want to stay friends then we can't talk about Silver Dove or the Crow anymore. I guess that I am alright with that for now, but one day I know she will support me as the Crow. She will realize that I am doing the right thing.

I turn to the second page, a blank page, and I begin to draw even though I have no idea what I plan on drawing. As I continue to sketch, my mind wanders. I think about what happened today, with Colomba reacting to my drawing and then me creating Tigerclaw and her battle with Silver Dove. I also think about what Nat had told us the other day on the bus about people wanting to form fan clubs for Silver Dove as well as for me. Maybe I should join my own fan club, I would love to see what my supporters think of me. I sigh and get that idea out of my head when I realize I can't do that. If I join that fan club then people might begin to tie things together and they might figure out that I am the Crow. I know that sounds like a long shot, but I can't be too careful about this. The other reason I can't join that club is because I know it would upset Colomba, and I never want to do that again. I never want to hurt her.

Before I know it, the drawing is finished. I smile faintly to myself when I see what I have drawn. Taking up the entire page is an image of Tigerclaw, her mouth is open wide in a ferocious growl, her fangs showing menacingly. Her claws are stretched out in front of her, getting ready to attack. Her fur covered face is an expression of rage that makes me smile. I know I messed up this first time, but I will try again, I have to. Closing my sketchbook, I place it in my backpack and start getting ready for bed. I need to get up early tomorrow. If I am going to defeat Silver Dove, then I am going to have to practice harder than before. I will not lose.

Chapter Twenty- Three

Colomba-
Martial Arts'
Newest Member

As I enter my martial arts studio, or dojo, I feel all of my stress melt away. No matter how bad I feel, that all goes away as soon as I come in here. Some of the other students are already here, talking casually, but I see the back of someone's head that I don't recognize. The mystery person is talking to Jeff, the instructor. When he sees me come in, Jeff smiles and gestures for me to come over to him and whoever he is talking to.

"Hey Colomba, I want you to come here and meet the newest member of our class." Walking over, I am both surprised and delighted by who I see.

"Hey there Jade Elizabeth. How are you?" She

smiles shyly at me, glancing up at me through her eyelashes.

"I'm fine." Jeff smiles at the two of us.

"I'll let you girls chat for a bit while I finish getting set up for class." He walks away while I continue speaking with Jade Elizabeth.

"What made you want to start taking martial arts with us?" She rubs her hands together, obviously nervous about explaining what she is about to say.

"Well when I was… taken over by the Crow, Silver Dove gave me some good advice." I feel my smile growing larger. "She said that if I want to be stronger than I am now, then I will have to work for it. I can't just expect to be strong immediately. I'm here to learn how to be stronger." She finally looks me straight in the eyes to see that I am staring at her with absolute joy.

"If you want to better yourself and make yourself stronger, then I am ready and willing to help you do that. Come on, I'll show you around the place." Leading her into the training area, I show her everything. I'm happy that our newest member is giving herself the chance to improve despite her fear, willing to work through that to become the person she wishes to be.

When I am through showing her around, Jeff starts the lesson and we both eagerly join the class. While I am helping Jeff with the class, I watch Jade

Elizabeth, smiling when I see that many of the other students are welcoming her to the class, talking to her kindly. Jade Elizabeth tries to forget her shyness as she answers their questions and joins in their conversations. She works hard during the class and in my heart, I know that she will become stronger here.

Jade Elizabeth's experience with Silver Dove and the Crow seems to have worked out for the best. She seems to have learned a few things about herself because of us. I think I have taught her that she is capable of helping herself, that she doesn't have to be as weak as she thought she was. From the corner of my eye, I watch as she becomes more and more comfortable around everyone here. I even see her beginning to smile. She may have been a difficult person to fight, but I am glad that I went through with it. Seeing that smile on her face has made all my time training and fighting as Silver Dove worth it. I wouldn't trade this feeling of pride and joy that I have right now for anything, not even all the gold in the world.

I try to pay attention to the other students as I help them, but my eyes keep getting drawn to our newest member. Nothing pleases me more than when I see someone beginning to enjoy martial arts when I help teach. It pleases me even more seeing that it is Jade Elizabeth, knowing everything she has gone through.

Before I know it, class is over, and everyone is filing out of the dojo. I walk beside Jade Elizabeth and start chatting with her, trying to be careful not to mention anything about her battle with Silver Dove. I don't want to accidently reveal anything that nobody besides Silver Dove would know. It would be a bit embarrassing to accidently reveal my true identity to someone I was fighting just the other day. I would feel like a complete dummy if I did that. I would have ended my career as Silver Dove when my career has only just started. We talk until her father and my grandmother come to pick us up. We both get in the separate cars, waving goodbye to each other before we are driven home.

Chapter Twenty- Four

Luis-
Next Time

I usually hate walking into school in the morning, knowing that I will probably get picked on by somebody. Today is different though, today I feel happy. I look around at everyone as I pass through the hallways. They are all talking about what happened yesterday with Tigerclaw and Silver Dove. They are afraid, they are afraid of me, and they should be. After everything that they have done to me, after making me afraid all these years, they deserve to be a little afraid too. I once heard someone say that revenge is taking an eye for an eye. Well for me, I am giving fear for all of the fear they gave me. I have heard many times that you shouldn't get revenge. That it is a terrible thing to do to anyone, no matter what they have done to you. Now I laugh when I think of that, whoever said that had obviously never taken revenge before. I am doing it, and right now I feel fantastic. I have never felt better in my life.

Just last night, only a few hours after the battle, I saw that someone had put up some mean things about a girl in one of my classes up on A-Streamer. Apparently, they still haven't learned what I have been trying to teach them. They can't pick on people without having some kind of consequences. For now, that consequence is me. If I have to keep using my powers to make these people realize that they can't pick on others, then I will gladly do that. I will do whatever it takes to make sure that the bullied kids like me get what they deserve, the chance to fight back.

Even though I haven't quite reached everyone yet, I can already see a lot of the bullied kids standing up a little taller now, no longer slouched over in fear. They know that I am here to help them, they know that soon they will never have to be afraid again. One day, everyone in the school will be kinder to each other. We won't have to worry about cliques and mean people, everyone will be happy. If I have to make everyone afraid to pick on each other to do that, then I am willing.

Up ahead of me, I see Colomba getting something out of her locker while she talks with Nat and someone else. My smile fades a little when I look at her. I know, even though she didn't say anything, that I scared her too. I scared the girl I care about. Closing my eyes for a moment, I lower my head, feeling ashamed. Colomba is such a kind and innocent girl, scaring a person like her is probably the worst thing I have ever done. I want to make this school better for everyone, including her. If I have to scare her a few times to get there, then I will do that. I wouldn't want her to become a victim of all the mean people in this school like I have. I raise my head again, trying to forget about my shame. I am doing something good for everyone. I shouldn't feel ashamed. I am the good guy here.

As I continue to walk toward Colomba, I suddenly stop when I notice the other person beside her, Jade Elizabeth, Tigerclaw. I didn't recognize her at first because she isn't wearing her signature hood. She isn't trying to hide her face, letting herself be exposed to the world. The two of them are talking with each other. Jade Elizabeth is actually talking to someone. Only a few days ago she would have run away if someone tried to talk to her, now she is talking to Colomba. How is this happening? Did I miss something? She still seems to be having trouble looking Colomba in the eyes when she talks, but she is at least talking to her. I stare at her with wide eyes; how is this possible? She refused my help and gave back the powers I gave her. How has she changed so much in just one day?

Taking a moment to think, I realize something. Maybe it's because of what I did for her that she is like this. Maybe since I gave her those powers and she had at least one day to take her revenge, maybe that gave her the confidence to come out of her shell a bit more. Maybe she didn't need as much time as I had thought she would. Maybe that one day was all she needed. I smile again, feeling proud of myself. I did that for her. I gave her the confidence to finally let the world hear her voice. I can only hope that the world won't try to silence her again.

Instead of going over there to join them in their conversation, I walk down a different hallway. I need some time alone to think, I have a plan to make. Things didn't work out too well with Tigerclaw, I need to be smarter about who I choose. I can't just pick any bullied kid, I need one who will do what I say, follow my orders so that we can accomplish what I set out to do, get rid of all the bullies. I need someone who understands why I need to do this. Apparently Jade Elizabeth wasn't that person. Well, if I have learned anything from art class, I know that you can never make a masterpiece on the first attempt. I will just have to try again. Maybe my next soldier won't disappoint me.

Don't miss The Adventure Begins, book 1.

Eliza Scalia is currently a Masters student for Clinical Mental Health at Troy University. She enjoys reading and needlework, as well as hanging out with her two pets, her dog Maggie and her cat Dusty. Eliza has been writing for many years and has self- published the Death's Assistant series for young adults.